Welcome Back, Class of '65

Brenda Crissman Musick

Jan-Carol
Publishing, Inc
"every story needs a book"

Welcome Back, Class of '65
Brenda Crissman Musick

Published October 2019
Little Creek Books
Imprint of Jan-Carol Publishing, Inc.
All rights reserved
Copyright © 2019 Brenda Crissman Musick

ISBN: 978-1-950895-22-9
Library of Congress Control Number: 2019952983

You may contact the publisher:
Jan-Carol Publishing, Inc.
PO Box 701
Johnson City, TN 37605
publisher@jancarolpublishing.com
jancarolpublishing.com

I chose the Class of '65 in my title
because that is the year I graduated.
The characters in this book
do not represent my classmates,
Well...not much anyway...
Maybe just a dab,
Not much at all,
Really...
Nevertheless, I would like to dedicate this book to MY Class of '65.
We were a close group of young men and women, and have remained close through
the years. I would like to dedicate it especially to Mary Ruth Elkins Patrick and
Carolyn Fletcher Puckett, two of the most courageous ladies I have ever known.

And as always, I dedicate this to my husband, the greatest of men.

In Memory

This book is in memory of my own Class of '65
classmates who are now deceased:

Jimmy Barrett Akers
Bobby "Bunk" Blankenship
Bobby Jack Cartwright
Freddy Coleman
Shirley Jackson Conley
Charlotte Taylor Ferguson
Carl "Pedro" Hale
Dennis Harris
Shelby Herndon
Barry Honaker
Brenda Faye McGlothlin Lambert
Wanda Martin
Jackie Steele
Ruth Jayne Boyd White

Letter to the Reader

This book has been two years in the making, with several detours along the way. In fact, it's the book I thought might never see the printed page. In early 2018, this book was about one-fourth of the way to completion. I had developed a cough that seemed to worsen daily. I always avoid doctors and medicine as much as possible, but finally I gave in and consulted my primary care physician. She sent me to another doctor, who sent me to another doctor, who sent me to another. You know how it goes. After a plethora of tests, two doctors decided I had walking pneumonia. The treatment? Antibiotics. My body rejected each kind. Eventually, after a second bronchoscopy, I heard the words that no one ever wants to hear:

"Mrs. Musick, you have primary lung cancer."

"How can I have lung cancer?" I asked. "I've never smoked a cigarette in my life."

The mass was a large one. In May, 2018, I underwent lung surgery, removing sixty-percent of my left lung. The surgeon assured me he had removed all of the mass, so I breathed a sigh of relief. That was over. On with life. He then sent me to see a medical oncologist as follow-up to the surgery. I wasn't sure what that was all about, but I agreed to it, telling myself it was just "normal procedure."

About five minutes into the office visit, the doctor mentioned chemotherapy. Now that word is almost as frightening as the word cancer. I immediately told him I didn't need or want chemotherapy.

"Mrs. Musick," he said, "the kind of cancer you have is known for its tendency to reappear. The chemotherapy would be extra assurance."

I remember the drive home that day. My husband and I spoke maybe five words. We were devastated. I was disappointed, scared, and, yes, angry. I had not given the oncologist my final answer as I had a lot of pondering and praying to do.

Finally, I consented and began treatments immediately. It was no fun. That's all I will say about chemo. Apparently it was not "extra assurance" either. With my next PET scan, there was cancer in my right lung. I then agreed to radiation treatments. That took care of the three nodules in my right lung, or so I thought. False relief. As I write this today, the cancer is back. Our next step? Undetermined.

With much effort, I did get this book written, and I am thankful for that. I hope my readers will enjoy it and that it will bring back special memories for them. School years are special. I have shared my health situation with you because there's something else I want to share. Through all of this, God has taught me so much. He has shown me what is important and what is not important. Material things are petty. Money comes and goes. What is important? God...family...friends...what you give while you are here. Life goes by so quickly. As I look back I smile, because I have been so richly blessed. At age eighteen I wasn't wise enough to pray and ask God who I should marry, but in His wisdom, God gave me the very best he had. I am so thankful for my children and grandchildren. What a blessing! What joy! And friends? Oh my! Friends have been there for me through it all. At times, I could actually feel their prayers. What does the future hold? None of us know that. But I know who is in control...and I am most blessed among women. I enjoyed several years of teaching, and I still teach bible studies. I've been able to write books, something that, until a few years ago, was just a dream. I have met so many interesting people through my writing. As you have talked with me about my books, you have told me your stories, and I loved hearing all of them. You have been one of my blessings. Thank you, dear readers, and God bless you.

Acknowledgments

School was always an important part of my life. I think that is true for most of us in one way or another. For some, it was a time of excitement, joy, maturing, and learning; for others a struggle. I loved learning and still do. I am an avid reader, and you will find me daily with a pencil in hand working crossword puzzles. What is my favorite T.V. program? Why, *Jeopardy*, of course, although I know very few of the answers. I teach Bible Studies at least twice a year. That requires a great deal of study and research, and I love every minute of it.

My high school years were special, affording a lifetime of memories. I was not a cheerleader. I was not Homecoming Queen. No, I was a bookworm. Nevertheless, I had a good time and our senior class is still dear to me. It is difficult to keep in touch with everyone, as we each get busy with life, but we've made valiant efforts with a degree of success. (Facebook helps.) Next year (2020) will make fifty-five years since graduation. Just saying that causes a lump in my throat and a tear in my eye. Where have the years gone? They do go so quickly. We had a forty-five-year reunion, but not a fifty-year as there was illness in the lives of many classmates, including mine. We are planning one next year, and I can't wait to see everyone. As shown in the dedication, fourteen classmates have passed away out of a class of sixty-two; some only in their twenties and thirties. They were courageous people, though, as are some still fighting health battles. I think country people are just born with courageous genes. Perhaps I'm biased, but those I know would seem to give authenticity to the statement. Shelby Herndon was one of the first to leave us. What a joy she was! We all loved her, and she was always upbeat and happy, though struggling with health problems even in her school years. Carl "Pedro" Hale was killed in a mining accident. He was always full of laughter, our Wittiest Class Boy, and he just made you feel good when you were around him. I won't name them all. That would be a book in itself, but they each have a special place in my heart.

Very few of our teachers are still living. We had some great ones; giants in my eyes. Two of them were influential in my decision to become a teacher. Dorothy Harrington was the ideal lady, soft-spoken but firm, who loved her profession. Carroll Wolfe, my senior English teacher, furthered my love of literature. After graduation, she became my friend and remains so today. Sexton Burkett was my algebra teacher. I never acquired a love for mathematics, but I had a great respect for him. He is still active in his church and community and is a special friend. My government teacher, Mrs. Arlene Buchanan was a terrific lady and teacher.

Though this book is not about my particular senior class, my classmates will relate to certain things in the book. Each class had some of the characters of this book. Some turned out just as we anticipated, others went in a totally different direction. We have our plans, but God has His too. I planned to go to college the spring after graduation and become a teacher. That plan was delayed nineteen years, but I finally made it, and it was just the right time. The school years were good years. It is my hope that each classmate will find something in this book to bring back a happy memory. There are many of them...from the days when we crossed that old railroad track.

Ready to Conquer

Look out world, here we come!
We'll walk these halls no more.
Diplomas in hand, tassels turned,
  Behind us clangs the door.

Look out world, we know it all!
We're ready to show our stuff.
We've passed the tests, endured the walk;
  We're determined and we're tough.

Look out world, we're brains and brawn!
We're nerds and football great.
From rocket science to the pros,
  We know the world can't wait.

Look out world, and good-bye school!
Teachers, we bid farewell.
We'll make our mark; you'll hear our names;
  No doubt, we will excel.

—Brenda Crissman Musick

Masonville, USA

It's just a small country town in the heart of the Central Appalachians, not much more than a bend in the road. The town is a part of the "Poverty Belt", though no one living there would consider it such, and would be put out if you called it that to their face. The residents of the town and its hills and hollows deem themselves rich, in the things that matter. Oh, they have little money—at least, most residents would fall into that category—but they are rich in the things that are important: love, family, friendship, and respect. Seldom does anyone there go on an exotic vacation; most don't even know what that is. A trip to the Smokies is a nice vacation for them, and a trip to the beach is living the high life. They do boast of a movie theater and a bowling alley, however, and then there's the lake not too many miles away where some take their boats...fishing boats, that is.

The town today is much like it was in 1965. Well, now most people have indoor plumbing, and very few have potbellied stoves (though there are a few). It's sort of like modernization flew over and tipped its hat, but the town said, "No thanks. Just be on your way." Folks there are leery of change. The coal industry, provider of most of the jobs, has broken backs and blackened lungs, but it afforded a living; it even made some rich. There's still coal there and those who want to work it, but the government has made so many regulations it's hard to keep the industry going. As a result, many are jobless. An abundance of farmers still live around Masonville, trying to eke out a living on any flat land they can find. They raise quite a bit of tobacco, although the government has just about wiped that out, too. They raise corn and hay for their cattle, and they still plant by the signs of nature. Some folks have moved away, looking elsewhere for jobs, while others have stayed, getting work here and there. In other words, the town is in limbo at best. Yet people hang on, because this is *their* town; this is *home*.

The little soda shop is no longer there, but in its heyday, it was a thriving, popular place where they made honest to goodness ice cream sundaes, with real ice cream, in real glass containers, and they didn't cost an arm and a leg. Mmm! Yum! Those who ate there can still taste them. Boys and girls came there every day after school to hang out, talk, and flirt. Mr. Anderson didn't mind, though. He was making money. There is a soda shop there today, but it doesn't hold a candle to the one in '65. It tries to look old, but it can't fool the home folk. Not much fools them. Then there was Doodle's Grocery Store. Oh, it was no Food City or Kroger's, but it had about anything a body could need. (I didn't say *want*.) There was a hardware store, a dime store, a little clothing store called Tanner's Clothing, and Bub's Grill, where you could get a bite to eat. They made the tastiest burgers you could find in the state: mouth-watering, fried up on a grill, bona fide beef burgers. There were also two gas stations, where they would fill it up for you *and* wash your windshield; they'd even check your oil if you asked, no extra charge. You can't get that nowadays. Sometimes *progress* is not *progress*. Masonville still has no traffic light. One would definitely come in handy, but no one is losing any sleep over getting one. You can't miss what you've never had. They go when it's clear and stop when it isn't...and they're content.

In 1965, however, it was a booming town—in its own way. The most well-known spot in Masonville was Masonville High School. You see, about everyone who lives in Masonville graduated from that very high school, and those coming on will do the same. Masonville High is the home of the Masonville Wildcats. Hooray!

We're gonna fight, fight, fight

For dear old Masonville!

We're gonna win this game!

You're doggone right we will!

For the great old school we love so well,

We're gonna win, win, yell, yell...Masonville!

Everyone raised in Masonville knows that school song by heart, and those who remained still sing it loudly at every ballgame. Many moved away after graduation, seeking the good life. Some found it, some didn't; some were never heard from again. Many classes get together at the old high school from time to time for a class reunion, so everybody can find out what everybody else has done with their life. That's where this story comes in. The class of '65 is having a class reunion at good ole Masonville High...the first in fifty years! Only a handful stayed on in Masonville, and they kept up with some of their classmates. Some haven't been heard tell of in fifty long years, but the reunion planners are determined to get in touch with every single classmate. After all, it is the age of the internet. The reunion planners committee consists of Betty Hartford Hill and her friend Cora Mae Davis.

What happened to the Most Likely to Succeed? Did they? Is the Most Athletic a coach somewhere in the sports world, with abs of steel and bulging muscles? Did he/she make it to the pros? What about the Most Intellectual? Did he/she become a rocket scientist, a doctor, or even a congressman maybe? One thing you can bank on: they each have their secrets! This could prove to be very interesting.

And so, the invitations went out...

You Are Invited

Betty Hartford Hill put the stamp on the last invitation, breathing a sigh of relief. She looked at the stack with equal feelings of excitement and trepidation. Fifty-two invitations! She had located every single one of the 62 graduates. Eleven had passed away, but she hoped to hear from their relatives she had managed to locate by internet.

I wonder how many will respond, she thought, picking up her wine glass. *Wouldn't it be amazing if everyone came? There was a time I wouldn't have responded. Now I want them all to see just how far "Poor Betty" has come. Oh, how I hate that name!* Her thoughts took her back to her school days. The taunting and bullying began in first grade, and had continued throughout high school.

"Poor Betty has a hole in her dress!" Susie Merle had called loudly. The other girls laughed and then began to chant, "Poor Betty has a hole in her dress! Poor Betty has a hole in her dress! Oh, what a mess! Oh, what a mess!"

She had held her head high, stuck her chin out, and walked away, but the kids had found their new favorite mode of entertainment, making fun of Poor Betty. She never told her parents; it wouldn't have done any good. Her father was a handyman who worked only when there was work. He was good at what he did, but certainly had no ambition. If he had a job waiting and decided he just wanted to stay home that day, then that's what he did. He received fewer and fewer job calls as people found him undependable. Her mother cleaned houses for people, but the jobs were erratic, depending on the needs of the "higher-ups." Betty had learned to do without the things other kids had, but she never learned to like it. Most of her clothes came from Goodwill or from out-of-town cousins. She never knew when she might wear a dress or blouse or skirt to school that had originally belonged to one of her classmates. *Oh, wouldn't they have had fun with that?!*

She had never had any real friends, no one to walk through the halls with, to confide in, to sit with at ballgames. Sometimes she and Sybil Grayson sat together at lunch, but that often made the bullying worse; Sybil was in the same boat as Betty, and had to put up with her share of the taunting. Neither had she ever had a boyfriend. Who would want to date Poor Betty Hartford?

It was after high school when Betty met Wallace Hill. He was ugly as homemade sin and lazy as they come, but he came from a decent family—and at least he was someone to date. She was working at a factory in town at the time, making almost nothing, and Wallace was manager of the factory. Several girls were "chasing" him, mostly because they thought he had money. From what she heard, he went out with quite a few—but when he started going with Betty, he had supposedly left the others behind. (That was a laugh.) When Wallace asked her to marry him, she agreed with little enthusiasm—and the lack of enthusiasm had remained—but Betty had a husband, and she was going to make something of him. It was Betty who had pushed him into real estate. The pay wasn't good at first, but he would be in the public eye more. Then the slot for mayor came open. She was determined that he would get the position, and she had worked hard to make it happen, even making a few deals "under the table."

Betty took another sip of wine and closed her eyes.

Now they'll all see how far I've come, she thought, a smile curling her lips.

She reached over to her kitchen sound system and pushed a button for some music.

"Pretty Woman, walking down the street. Pretty woman, the kind I'd like to meet..."

Yes, this would be her night. She would be the pretty woman at this reunion!

Millie Davis Cunningham stood looking down at the invitation she had just retrieved from the mailbox. A tear slid hesitantly from her eye.

You are cordially invited to our Fifty-Year Class Reunion at Masonville High School.

Fifty years! She looked up from the invitation and into the mirror that had hung for about that long in her foyer. Fifty years! *I look every day of it and more,* she thought as she gazed at herself, pushing back a strand of dull, brown-gray hair. *How on earth can I face my classmates? I look seventy-eight instead of sixty-eight! And what do I have to show for those years? I was voted Most Likely to Succeed. Yep, Millie Davis Cunningham, Most Likely to Succeed. What have I succeeded at? Getting married and having babies? I excel at washing clothes, mopping floors, and cleaning up everybody's messes. Can't wait to tell that to the Class of '65!" Listen, fellow students, today I mopped the kitchen floor. Yesterday, I washed three loads of clothes." I am a true success story.*

Millie walked into the kitchen and tossed the invitation on the counter. She had promised to make Dan a chocolate pie today, and she didn't even have the breakfast dishes washed. Why? Because she had to take the stupid dog to the vet, after it upchucked on the carpet three times! It was supposed to be Dan's dog, but she always ended up doing everything for it. She had also promised to go down to the hardware store this afternoon and work on the invoices. Wiping angrily at unwanted tears with the back of her hand, she thought, *No time for this gal to go to a class reunion.* With a shake of her head she grabbed a tissue. The hot water ran into the sink as she added Ivory Liquid. Glasses first, silverware second, then on to the dishes. This had been her routine for almost fifty years. Everything in her life seemed to be a routine. She had married Dan Cunningham just two months after graduation, and they had begun their married life in the same little brick ranch-style house where they still lived. Oh, they had done a lot of work on it, but it hadn't gotten any larger. It was still three bedrooms, one bath, living room and dining/kitchen combined. *Most Likely to Succeed! Yeah, sure!*

Millie turned from her dish washing, dried her hands, and picked up the invitation again.

Who is getting this together? Yeah, I might have known: Betty Hill, a.k.a. Betty Hartford. Good ole dependable Betty, Mayor of Masonville. Well, her husband was actually the mayor, but Betty pretty well ran the town. Who would ever have thought? Betty sure didn't grow up in any kind of wealth. She was known by most as Poor Betty Hartford, although Millie had never called her that. Her parents would have skinned her alive if they heard of her calling people names. She could even have felt sorry for Betty if Betty had tried to be more likeable, but she seemed to thrive on being the girl nobody liked. She couldn't remember Betty trying to make friends with anyone, or trying to change the way people thought of her. Most of the time she stuck her head up in the air and gave everyone a resentful look. It was only after she married that things began to change for Betty. Not that Millie begrudged Betty her success. It was just hard to like Betty sometimes. *Shame on you, Millie Cunningham!*

She scanned on down the page. The reunion would be held at the Masonville High School Cafeteria, June 18 at six o'clock. Pictures of the old cafeteria came flooding back. Dan had been sent to the principal's office for holding her hand in that cafeteria. She remembered Mrs. Miller's wonderful rolls, and Miss Stinson's banana pudding. Oh, sure, she had been in it many times in later years with her own children, but her mind pictured it the night of the Senior Prom when she danced every dance with Dan. My, how handsome he had been! Millie continued to read. There was to be a meal, dancing and a time for sharing.

Oh, boy! A time for sharing! That means get up and tell everyone about all of your accomplishments! Well, what if you haven't accomplished anything except having babies, keeping house, and trying to keep a hardware business above water?

Suddenly Millie felt shame wash over her. She should be thankful for a good marriage and the finest husband anyone could ask for. He had been faithful, dependable, and loving for fifty years. He had worked hard to provide for his family and was respected by everyone in town. He was active in their little church, and had been a deacon for more years than she could count. She could wear old gray sweats, her hair up in a ponytail and no makeup, and Dan would tell her how pretty she was. Millie smiled in spite of herself. They had two daughters who had always been a blessing to them. Rebekah was a wife, mother, and elementary school teacher; Sarah was a wife, mother, and nurse. Both had good marriages, and they had given Millie and Dan five magnificent grandchildren. Sarah's son Lane was autistic, but he had brought so much joy to the entire family. He was the only grandson, and they adored him.

Millie had grown up in a wonderful home. They didn't have a lot of money, but they sure had love. Her father worked for the Department of Transportation, not a high paying job but dependable and steady. Her mom had never worked outside the home. With five children there was no time for that, although the money would have helped. She cooked, cleaned, took care of a large garden, and canned food as it came in season. On top of that, she made most of the clothes Millie and her two older sisters wore. They always attended school events and supported their children. Both parents had gone on to their reward now, but they had been respected by the community. Her dad had been Sunday School Superintendent down at Masonville Baptist Church, and her mother was always cooking food and taking it to someone in need or someone who had lost a loved one. Yes, Millie had much for which to be thankful. She just wished she had accomplished something worthy of the title Most Likely to Succeed.

Millie switched on the radio beside the sink. It was set for WKMK as usual, the station that played oldies. Once more, she looked at the invitation. *Deadline: May 1, 2015. Tickets $25.00 per person. Bring any pictures you may have of school days and your family. Tell us about yourself these past fifty years, so we can put it in the booklet for everyone. Hope to see you one and all!*

She had to smile as the radio played the song that had been her and Dan's favorite:

Chapel of Love by the Dixie Cups.

Was the radio trying to tell her something?

In Chicago, **Bunn Morris** switched the sign on the door of his bar and grill to *Closed*. It was eleven p.m. and he was tired. He sat down at one of the tables with a drink in his hand, put his feet on the table, and let his 300-plus-pound body fill the chair. He wasn't much to drink, just felt it was good for business to carry one around. Sometimes he carried the same one all day long. He had just never acquired a taste for the stuff, and that was a blessing. He pulled the mail over to him as he lit his thirtieth (roughly) cigarette of the day. *Bunn old boy, these things can kill you,* he thought to himself. Then he laughed and took another puff. *Gotta die some way. Let's see, how many bills do I have today?* He grimaced as he ruffled through them. *One, two...what in the...*

Bunn couldn't believe his eyes. A letter of some sort had a return address in *Masonville*, his old hometown. He hadn't heard from anyone there in years. His dad and brother had moved away two years after he graduated, and he had no other family there anymore. Well, there was Aunt Jenny, his dad's sister. *Golly, she must be in her nineties now, if she's still living.* Bunn hadn't kept up with her, although at one time they were very close. After his mother died, Aunt Jenny had been the one he always turned to, the only one who seemed to give a hoot whether he lived or died. When he left, though, he left everything and everyone behind. Memories came flooding in as he stared at the envelope. *Football star Bunn Morris! Star quarterback Bunn Morris! Basketball star! Baseball star! Ladies' man Bunn Morris! Jock of Masonville High Bunn Morris!*

Bunn laughed out loud. That was fifty years ago. The people he knew in Chicago would die laughing to hear those titles applied to him.

Voted Most Athletic and Model Classman! The irony of that made him laugh again, but it was far from a joyful laugh.

"There is nothing athletic about *this* old guy," he said, "and Bunn, old boy, you are not a model for anything...except maybe a screw-up."

Open the stupid envelope, you fat dimwit.

He slid a steak knife along the closure, pulled out the single sheet of paper, and unfolded it cautiously.

You are cordially invited to our Fifty-Year Class Reunion at Masonville High School.

In spite of himself, his mouth dropped open. He continued to stare at the paper. Suddenly, as though pulling himself from another world, he tossed the paper on the table.

"Fat chance!" he exclaimed.

He hefted his body from the chair and walked over to the jukebox, placing both hands on it. For a moment, Bunn just stood there, his thoughts roiling. A perceptive onlooker might have detected a tear in his eye, though he would never have admitted it. Finally, looking over the selections, his eyes fell on a song from the Sixties. He punched it in and went back to his seat as Roger Miller belted out, "Dang me, dang me. They oughta take a rope and hang me..."

"I can relate to that," Bunn said to the walls. "That's what I deserve."

He took another draw and puffed out a ring of smoke. This time, there was no mistaking the tears.

It had been a long day at the office for **Audra James**, and she was tired. As was her routine, she withdrew the mail from the box beside her door, then unlocked the door to her apartment and entered. She laid the mail on the table in the foyer, kicked off her four-inch champagne beige heels, and felt her body relax. She looked in the mirror over the table.

You have tired lines around your eyes, Audra. Not good. You'll need to use extra eye cream tonight. It may be time for more Botox.

No one in the office would guess she was sixty-eight years old. Most thought she was in her forties. Smiling sadly, she said to her reflection in the mirror, "You've paid large prices to look that way, Audra old girl."

She had never exactly lied about her age, but she saw no need to declare it to the world, either. Picking up the mail again, she walked on to the kitchen and poured herself a glass of wine. Then she went to her outdated stereo system to choose some soothing classical music to help her relax. As she leafed through her CDs, her eyes fell on one she hadn't played in years.

Wow, the Righteous Brothers! "You've Lost That Loving Feelin'." I haven't played that in decades.

She liked to stick to classical. It was more in keeping with the "new" Audra, the Audra she became after she left Masonville. After staring at it a moment longer, she put the CD in the player and headed to the couch with the mail and her glass of wine.

"You've lost that lovin' feelin', whoa that lovin' feelin'..."

She had to smile to herself. *If my old man heard me playing that, he would turn over in his grave,* she thought. *Maybe that's why I like it so much. I like anything he hated, and I hate anything he liked.*

With the smile still on her face, she sorted through her mail. Then one envelope caught her eye and she gasped. Her heart began to pound.

Speak of the dead!

The return address was one she hadn't seen in years: Masonville, the town where she'd grown up. *And boy, did I grow up,* she thought. The memories, long forbidden, came roaring back. She shook her head, trying to drive them away. Without even wanting to do so, Audra tore open the envelope and unfolded the paper.

You are cordially invited to our Fifty-Year Class Reunion at Masonville High School, she read.

Then the tears came. She couldn't stop them, or the memories that followed. Both came in torrents, roaring and screaming and tearing at the heart she had built walls around years ago. No one had ever been allowed inside those walls, and they never would be. Those walls harbored horrible secrets; *no one* was allowed inside to see them. She held her head in her hands trying to make the memories go away. The pain was not due to memories of her old high school, though; it was the *other* memories that were agonizing.

"I can't go back there," she sobbed. "I just *can't.*" Tears soaked the invitation as the CD played.

"You've lost that lovin' feelin', whoa, that lovin' feelin'..."

What loving feeling? She didn't even know what love was supposed to feel like. She only knew about sadness and fear and pain and hate. Her parents had certainly never loved her; love could not coexist with so much anger and abuse. Love and the devil could not live together. Love had no part in the things they had done to her.

Pushing back the S & S cap on his head, **Harmon Cline** locked the door of his office. Before turning to go, he looked at the name on the door, *Slade and Son Trucking.* Forty-five years ago, life had finally dealt him a decent hand. He walked away laughing, and as he opened the door of his Dodge Ram pickup, he tossed the day's mail across to the passenger's seat, lit up a cigar, and started the truck. He used to smoke cigarettes, but now cigars seemed more fitting to his position.

I wonder what Rosalee is fixing for dinner, he mused. *Luckiest day of my life was when I met that woman, and the second luckiest was when I married her. She's one in a million...and she came with a bonus!* Not that he had married her for the bonus. He loved that woman with every fiber of his being. The highlight of his day was going home and taking Rosalee in his arms. Even at 64, she was the most beautiful woman he had ever seen, and she was honest. You always knew where you stood with Rosalee.

He reached over to straighten the mail before it slid between the seats. As he retrieved the one near the edge, his eyes widened. "Holy..." he said. "What on earth? *Masonville?* Lord, I haven't thought about that place in years!"

He gripped the cigar between his teeth and tore open the envelope in his usual crude manner. He had never used a letter-opener. *Real men don't use letter openers,* he thought, smiling. *Those are for sissies.* He unfolded the single sheet of paper.

You are cordially invited to our Fifty-Year Class Reunion at Masonville High School.

Harm almost dropped the cigar from his mouth. He didn't know whether to laugh or cuss. Why would he want to go back there? Those country hicks had looked down their noses at him every day of his life because he was from the wrong side of the tracks and poor as a church mouse.

It didn't matter that my mama worked her fingers to the bone to provide a living for herself and her son, while the other "good" women of Masonville sat in beauty parlors with cucumbers on their eyes, gossiping. It didn't matter that she loved her son and showed it every day. It didn't matter that she read her Bible and taught her son right from wrong. No, it only mattered that I didn't have a daddy—or at least I didn't know who he was. One mistake, and the town never forgot it! Those fine so-called Christian folks never forgot her mistake, and constantly let him know *he* was the mistake. *Fat chance I'll go back there!*

You did have some good times at school, an inner voice seemed to say to him.

Yes, he had had some good high school years, especially in sports. He was a good basketball player because of his lanky six-foot-four frame, not to mention the agility. He was a pretty fair baseball and football player. *Bunn Morris...now, that was a football player if ever there was one,* he mused.

Bunn was always good to him, too. He wondered how Bunn did after high school. If he made the pros, Harm had never heard about it. Of course, he'd spent a good bit of time in Guam and Vietnam, and didn't keep up with the news back home.

No, there is no need for me to go back to Masonville and the past. Mama is gone now, after losing her painful battle with ovarian cancer, so there is nothing there for me.

On the other hand...

Ole Harm ain't a poor church mouse from the wrong side of the tracks anymore! He laughed and chewed on his cigar. *Wonder what they would say if they knew Ole Harm made it big? Wonder if they wouldn't just wet their pants to find out the mistake boy with no daddy is now worth millions? Why, those gossipy ole biddies would drop their cucumbers! It might be worth going back just to see the looks on their faces.*

Nah...

He turned his truck radio on from his steering wheel.

"Since I met you baby, my whole life has changed..."

He loved that song because it told his life story. When he met his beautiful Rosalee, his whole life changed. They had never been able to have children, and he missed that part of life, but they had each other and life was good.

Letting himself into his dinky little apartment in a rundown tenant building in upper Ohio, **Wilson Baker** rubbed his aching back. Loading and unloading crates all day long was a hard job, but he was lucky to have one. He threw his keys and the two pieces of mail that had been pushed under the door onto the rickety table beside the ratty old couch and headed to the fridge for a cold beer. As he opened the door, he shook his head. An almost empty pack of bologna, part of a jar of mayo, and two beers made up its entire contents. Those would be gone by bedtime. He would have to find time to get a few things after work tomorrow, with what little money he had left until payday. He had managed to buy a small television a couple of months ago. The screen was so small you had to squint to see the picture, but at least it provided some entertainment to ease the silence that raged at him each night. He switched it on and took a long swig of beer, stretching out on the couch to ease his back. Before long he was snoring.

It was nine o'clock when Willie awoke. The beer still in the can was warm, but he drank it anyway. *Guess I'll make myself a gourmet bologna sandwich,* he thought, getting up from the couch. He found what was left of a loaf of bread. It was beginning to mold, but he simply tore off the molded part and spread each piece with mayo. Opening his last can of beer with sandwich in hand, he headed back to the couch. As he set the beer on the side table, he noticed the two pieces of mail he had brought in. One was advertising a new cable company; the other...

Well, cut off my legs and call me Shorty, he thought as he looked at the return address...*Masonville. My old alma mater! Boy, did we have some great times there!*

The letter had been forwarded to him from his sister Carolyn in Baxter. With overwhelming curiosity, Willie opened the envelope, unfolded the paper inside, and read:

You are cordially invited to our Fifty-Year Class Reunion at Masonville High School.

He leaned back against the threadbare couch cushion, stunned. *Why on earth are they having a reunion? They've never had one before, as far as I know—but then they might not have known where to send my mail. As far as I know, no one there knew where I was; but then, how did they get Carolyn's address? Probably the internet; you can find anything there. Wonder what else they found out?*

The television was still playing and his beer and sandwich still lay on the table, but Willie Baker was lost in thought, going back to another place and another time. He leaned his head back and allowed the memories to come.

Wilson Baker, Most Likely to Succeed.

Boy, had he succeeded!

"They should see all of my success," he said to the walls. "I live in a building that could fall apart at any moment or go up in flames if I dropped a cigarette. I have a job that barely keeps me going. I'm afraid to sleep most nights because of the nightmares...Lord what nightmares. I have no friends, no family except for my sis, and oh yeah... Willie Baker, *Most Likely to Succeed,* just got out of prison! That should make for some lively conversation!"

Nope! Don't think they'll see old Willie at the fiftieth reunion.

He switched the TV over to the Golden Oldies channel.

"I'm sittin' on the dock of the bay, watching the tide roll away. I'm sittin' on the dock of the bay wastin' time..."

Yep. That was him, just sitting around waiting as life went slowly by.

A car backfired in the alley below his window, and Willie dived for the floor.

Sybil Grayson Welles looked at her fingernails and frowned.

"Darn! Another chip, and I had them done only yesterday."

She rang the little bell on the huge kitchen island and called out, "Martha, would you call and ask Deidre to send one of the girls up to fix my nails? I can't go to the Eldridge's party tonight with chipped polish."

"Yes, ma'am," replied Martha, coming in from the laundry room. "Oh, I put your mail on your dresser, Mrs. Welles."

Sybil didn't bother to reply. She was much too busy trying to decide what to wear to the party. Arthur's tux had arrived an hour ago, and now she needed to pick something that looked like a million dollars—but also like she'd just pulled it out at the last minute. She had learned long ago how to play these social games.

"Maybe this red one," she mused aloud. "I bought this the last time we were in Italy, and I've never worn it. It shows off my figure divinely."

She held it up in front of herself and viewed the effect in the mirror, then laid it carefully on the bed. She gave her hair a pat.

It's still thick with body, she thought proudly. *Teresa always does such a good job with the color. I made a wise decision when I moved her to my New York City salon. Soon I'll make her the manager of all my New York stores. She's earned the position. I'll still expect her to do my hair when I'm in the city, though.*

Sybil's eyes traveled down her body. All the lifts and tucks had paid off. She had a young and attractive body for a woman of 68. No one would have guessed her age. Arthur appreciated beauty, and she always tried to please him. After all these years and a few problems, she still loved him.

As she turned from the mirror, she glimpsed the mail on the dresser where Martha had neatly placed it. Martha knew how much Sybil liked neatness. She picked up the stack and carried it to the little divan near the penthouse window.

Hmm... Sybil glanced from one envelope to the other. Several were party and dinner invitations. She and Arthur were a vibrant part of New York City's social scene.

As she came to a slightly crumpled envelope, she moaned. Without even looking at the return address, she knew who it was from; Herb Grayson, her no-good bum of a father. No doubt he wanted money. At least twice a year he would send a letter crying over his financial situation. *Lousy bum! He drinks and gambles it away, then expects me to refill his wallet.*

The trouble was, her father knew she would do it. If she refused, he might show up on her doorstep; she couldn't have *that.* She would be mortified to have any of their social acquaintances or friends know about her childhood life and the louse she still had for a father. She had endured so much because of him, especially the taunting and ridicule in school. She had never had pretty clothes. Feed sack skirts and dresses had made up her wardrobe. She went hungry more times than she could even count, all because of her no-good bum of a father. For as long as she could remember, her father had been a gambler and a sot. Since her mother had no backbone, Sybil had spent her childhood and teen years trying to hide their weaknesses. And now he expected her to keep him up. Arthur didn't even know about the money she gave her father just to keep him away. Neither did he know how she had grown up.

Sybil tossed the letter in her lingerie drawer. She would deal with it later. Then as her eyes caught the return address on the last piece of mail, her heart began to race. *Masonville! Oh, my heavens! I left that little hick town behind me long ago.*

For awhile she stared at the return address, color traveling from her neck to her face. Then she sighed and ran her ivory-handled letter opener along the top. Unfolding the paper with shaky hands, she read:

You are cordially invited to our Fifty-Year Class Reunion at Masonville High School.

Sybil swallowed. *A fifty-year reunion. Fifty years! Where has time gone?*

She folded the letter, put it back in the envelope, and carefully placed it with the other envelope in her lingerie drawer. She could never go back there. She was a nobody there, and she could never go back to being a nobody. Sybil had kept in touch with only one person connected to Masonville, and no one could ever know about that. That was another reason she couldn't go back.

No way! Not in a million years! But if they only knew how far I've come...

Then Sybil's haughty pride began to take over. *Oh, wouldn't they be green with envy to know what I have accomplished for myself! They would be so jealous to see me walk in on the arm of Arthur Welles. He's twelve years my junior, but he makes me look younger. I see the look in women's eyes when we walk into a party or dinner. Yes, he has strayed a few times...but he always comes back to me, and he makes me feel beautiful and important. I'm no longer Sybil Grayson, daughter of the town bum. When he looks into my eyes, I'm a queen.*

Sybil looked again at the invitation. It was tempting. No. It had been too long, and there were too many memories in Masonville, memories better left alone. But still...

The lyrics from one of her favorite songs popped into her mind. *Ain't no mountain high enough; ain't no valley low enough; ain't no river wide enough, to keep me from getting to you...*

Sybil hummed to herself as she went back to shoes and dress choices. Then she began to sing the words.

"Ain't no mountain high enough... Ain't no valley low enough..."

To Go
or
Not to Go?

Betty Hartford Hill sorted through the mail Wallace had brought home and laid on the kitchen bar. *No replies to the invitations. Oh well, I suppose it is a little too soon. I can't wait to see who comes, or who at least sends some information. Thanks to me, we found addresses for one hundred percent of the classmates. Okay, so Wallace's secretary helped! No one else knew that.*

Betty poured herself another glass of wine. Wallace told her she drank too much, but she knew she could handle it. She just felt better with a glass in her hand, a little more sophisticated. She had her plans for the reunion laid out on the table in front of her. Beside them was her 1965 yearbook. She had to use it to put faces to all the names after fifty years, and to make the name tags. She often sat for hours looking at each face, wondering what they had become.

Millie Davis Cunningham. Why, she lives right here in Masonville! Nice enough, but a nobody. Bunn Davis. Wow! He was handsome and popular, but he never noticed girls like me. Audra James. Mousey little girl. Her father was some kind of a preacher. Dorothy Cartwell. Oh yeah, her father owned some mines. Rather wealthy. Can't remember much about her.

Betty had gone through the pictures and names dozens of times as she planned the reunion in detail. Most of the plans were her plans. Well, actually *all* of them were, but she tried to give Cora credit for some of them. Cora Mae Davis had mostly been her sounding board. She usually agreed with everything Betty said.

I have to make her think she's helping, mused Betty, with a wicked smile. *Later she can help with the physical labor. She thinks I consider her my best friend, but that's a joke. I know things she doesn't think I know, and one day, when the time is just right, it will all come out.*

Sorting through the papers listing the decorations, Betty took another sip of wine, enjoying the tingle as it warmed her throat. Her classmates would see just how far she had come since 1965. She was no longer Poor Betty, or the handyman's daughter. She was married to the mayor of Masonville, Wallace Hill, who was also a real estate executive—that's the way Betty referred to his job, at least. Actually, he just sold real estate once in awhile. The market in Masonville wasn't exactly booming.

Not that he's any big catch, she thought, grimacing. *He's dumb as mud, and has no ambition. If it wasn't for me, he couldn't make a single decision for this town; not to mention I've written every speech he's ever made. I'm the real mayor, and who knows? One day I may officially have that title.*

Had she ever loved Wallace? Not really. She mostly loved the fact that he came from a well-respected, "old money" family. To her chagrin, when Wallace's father died, they had discovered that most of the money had been used up. He left his family nothing but a few debts. At least Mr. Hill had been a man of gumption, something his son had certainly not inherited. He didn't have a lot of brains, either. That was okay, though; Betty had enough brains and ambition for both of them.

Betty looked in the mirror in the hallway. She was not gorgeous, but no one could deny her elegance. She dressed elegantly and carried herself elegantly. That was something her mother-in-law, Gladys Hill, had taught her. One would never find her without makeup, hair a mess, or in sweats. No, siree! She never even went out without jewelry. She had a right to spend money on clothes, makeup, and spas. After all, she was the "woman behind the man." She had an image to keep up. She had put Poor Betty behind her, the Betty Hartford who wore Goodwill clothes and had barely enough food to eat. Her handyman father had died years ago, and her mother was stashed safely away in a nursing home in Baxter, where she wouldn't be an embarrassment. She didn't know where her younger brother was, nor did she care. She didn't want anyone from the past to taint the new life she had built for herself.

As she delved into her memories, Betty walked over to her state-of-the-art music nook and touched the light for her favorite song.

"Pretty woman, walking down the street. Pretty woman, the kind I'd like to meet..."

Betty looked in the mirror once more and patted her face.

She and Wallace had bought a beautiful home about twenty years ago, the largest, she was sure, in all of Masonville. It was mortgaged to the hilt, but that wasn't anyone's business but theirs. They had mortgaged it through a bank in Craigsville, over a hundred miles away, so that no one in Masonville would know. Betty and Wallace had two grown, affluent sons (at least on the surface): Murphy, a lawyer, and Marcus, a banker. Their wives were a part of Masonville's society set. She couldn't abide either of her daughters-in-law, but that was neither here nor there. As far as the people in town knew, she adored them. Marcus and Melanie had no children, nor did they want any, thank God; but Murphy and Elaina had two sons, rowdy, insolent children that she rarely saw. Murphy drank to excess, and Betty just hoped he wouldn't let it ruin his career.

"Our son is a lush, Betty," Wallace had declared just the night before. "He's a full-blown lush, and you might as well accept the fact."

"He will be fine, Wallace," she said, dismissing the truth of his statement as she took another sip of wine. "He has a lot on his plate right now, and living with Elaina is enough to drive anyone to drink. She does nothing but spend money and go to spas."

She didn't miss the accusatory look Wallace gave her, but chose to ignore it with another sip. He then went off to his study and Betty spent the evening going over her plans once more.

I really need to take off a few pounds before the reunion, and maybe I'll have a few injections around my eyes.

She looked at the plans for the decorations again, making sure for the hundredth time she hadn't left out anything important.

I'll be sure to greet everyone at the door, she thought, a twinkle in her eyes. *They'll see right off just how far Betty Hartford Hill, the First Lady of Masonville, has come. I know I look better than the ones who have remained in Masonville. Cora looks her age and more, with that sagging wrinkled neck! And she's had a limp since her hip surgery. What he sees in her..? Then there's Millie Cunningham. She has a nice figure, but her clothes are cheap and she never wears makeup. Then they have that grandson...* She thought of several others living in Masonville, and a few she had found on Facebook. She could outshine all of them with her hands tied behind her. She would make them forget about Poor Betty Hartford.

"Pretty woman, walking down the street..."
Betty patted her hair and smiled.

Millie had pushed that one piece of broccoli around on her plate for the last fifteen minutes. She knew Dan was talking, but her mind was miles away...well, a few blocks anyway.

"And I invited fifty people to spend the weekend with us. Is that OK with you, Hon?" Dan asked.

"Uh-huh," she replied.

Dan reached over and placed his hand on hers. "Mil, you haven't heard a thing I've said tonight. Is something wrong?"

"Why, sure I've heard you," said Millie.

"Then it is really OK if I've invited fifty people to spend the weekend with us?" he asked, a twinkle in his eye.

"Fifty people?! What are you talking about, Dan Cunningham?"

"That's what I asked you, and you said 'Uh-huh', so that must mean it's all right."

"You're teasing me, aren't you?" she said, giving him a weak smile. "I'm sorry, Dan. I guess I was just thinking about all the invoices I need to take care of."

Shame on you, Millie Cunningham. You just lied to your husband.

Dan looked at her for a moment. "Are you sure that's all it is? Are you upset about something? Are the kids OK?"

Millie squeezed his hand. "Everything is fine, Dan. I'm sorry. Guess I'm just a little out of it tonight."

"Millie, if it's getting to be too much for you to do the invoices at the store, I think we could afford to hire someone a couple of days a week."

She felt about an inch tall. "Absolutely not! I love coming down to the store. It gets me out of the house for a while, and I can spy on you, too."

Dan continued to look at her, concern obvious in his eyes. Then he leaned over and kissed her. "I love you, my beautiful bride."

Tears sprang to her eyes. "Oh, Dan, look at me. I could never pass for a bride."

"You will always be my bride."

"Dan, do you ever wish we had moved from Masonville?"

His eyes widened. "Move from Masonville? Golly, no! I love this town and our life here. Why would you ask that?"

"I don't know. Sometimes I just wonder, I guess. Do you wish I had gone on and gotten a better education so I could help with the finances?"

Dan, drew back and looked into Millie's eyes. "What has brought all of this on, Mil? Are you worried about money? Are you unhappy with me?"

"No! No, of course not."

"Well, let me set your mind at rest, Millie Davis Cunningham. I am as happy as a pig in a mud pile. You and the girls are everything to me, and there's never been a day of our marriage that I haven't felt blessed. We have two beautiful and loving daughters who married fine men, and the smartest grandchildren in the entire town—if not the entire state."

Millie smiled. "How did I ever luck into a man like you, Dan Cunningham?"

"Guess you're just lucky," he replied, planting another kiss smack dab on her lips.

The next morning as Millie was doing the breakfast dishes, she heard a light knock on the kitchen door and Sarah peeped in, the usual happy smile on her face.

"Come in, Sarah," said Millie, wiping her hands on the dish towel. "What brings you by this early in the morning?"

Sarah gave her mother a hug. "Well, I have two days off and I'm headed to the grocery store, but first I wanted to stop by and see my darling mother. Wanna go with me?"

"I just might. I am in need of a few things, but first have a cup of coffee and chat with me while I finish these dishes."

Sarah poured herself a cup of coffee. "Now, what is that I see to the left of the sink, Mom? Oh, yes...I know! That's what they call a *dishwasher*. I think they are for washing dishes."

"I know what it's for," replied her mother. "I just happen to like standing here at the window, washing my dishes and watching the birds. Now stop being feisty, and tell me about my grandchildren."

For the next twenty minutes, the two women chatted happily.

Sarah emptied her cup into the sink and washed it before setting it in the drainer. "Go get ready now, Mom. I have lots to do today."

Millie headed to the bedroom and Sarah sat at the island reading the daily newspaper. As she moved it, a letter fell to the floor and she bent to retrieve it. She couldn't help but see the first line.

You are cordially invited to our Fifty-Year Class Reunion at Masonville High School.

Just then her mother returned, ready to go.

"Mom," said Sarah, "you didn't tell me you are having a class reunion. That's exciting, after fifty years."

Millie couldn't stop the flush of her face. "Oh, I haven't told anyone, dear. I don't think I want to go."

"Don't want to go? Why on earth not? You live right here. Oh, Mom, I think it will be lots of fun seeing old classmates and finding out about everyone. Many still live here, don't they?"

Millie sat down on the barstool. "Yes, I suppose some do. But Sarah, many of them have accomplished so much in those fifty years, and look at me. I'm just a...a housewife."

She immediately regretted her words as tears came to Sarah's eyes.

"Is that so bad, Mom? I always felt like you were happy with Dad, Rebekah, and me."

Millie pulled Sarah to her. "My darling, I am happy, and I am so proud of my daughters and my grandchildren. It's *me* I'm not happy with. Look at me: I'm twenty pounds overweight, with mousey hair; it's half brown, half gray. I don't have a college degree. I've lived in the same house for fifty years. I've hardly been out of the state, and I was voted Most Likely to Succeed."

Sarah placed her hands on her hips like she had done as a little girl when she was angry.

"Mom, you are the most accomplished woman I know! You are the most fantastic mother and grandmother in the entire universe...and you are *going* to that reunion! We are going to get you ready, beginning today. First, we are going to see if Mazie has any openings at the beauty parlor. By the way, what does Dad say about the reunion?"

"I haven't told him," answered Millie, a sheepish look on her face.

"Mom!" thundered Sarah, hands back on her hips. "What am I going to do with you?"

"I thought you said you have a lot to do today, Sarah. You don't have time to go to a beauty parlor with me."

"I most certainly do! I can't think of anything more important, and it will be fun. Other things can just wait. How many times have you put other things aside for Rebekah or me, or even your grandchildren? A makeover for my mom! You'll be the most beautiful woman at the reunion. Now let's go!"

"I will go to the beauty parlor," groaned Millie, "but I am not agreeing to go to the reunion yet. We'll see."

"We certainly will," said Sarah, a stubborn set to her jaw.

Thus began Millie's makeover. When one of her daughters got a bee in her bonnet, there was no stopping her. By the end of the day, she had a new hairstyle and a new color. She had to admit, it did look rather nice. Sarah dropped her off at the hardware store afterwards to work on the invoices, with an adamant assurance that both she and Rebekah would be at the house by nine o'clock the following morning to begin the next makeover phase, and it would include exercise. Millie did not look forward to that. She hated exercise.

"Mother!" Sarah called, just before she pulled away from the curb. "Tell Dad!"

As she left Sarah's car and headed toward the store, Dan was just putting some wheelbarrows outside for display. He looked at her, turned back to the display, then stopped in his tracks.

"Millie?"

It was all he could say.

She was smiling her most mischievous smile.

"Millie, is that you?"

"Dan Cunningham, we have been married fifty years. Are you telling me you don't know me?"

"What have you done to yourself?"

"Don't you like it?"

"You are absolutely beautiful!"

Millie glowed with his praise. *Thank you, my darling Sarah!*

"What brought this about?" Dan asked, leaning down to give her a kiss. "You don't have another man I don't know about, do you?"

"Oh, several," she teased. "But you're still my number one."

He still looked perplexed.

"Your youngest daughter came by this morning, and after listening to me bewail my dull, mousey hair, she insisted on taking me to the salon. I kinda like it."

Millie spent the afternoon doing invoices and then headed home to prepare supper. She would tell Dan about the reunion after they ate.

Opening the door to his apartment atop the bar and grill, **Bunn** flipped on the light and headed for the kitchen, tossing the mail on the already crowded coffee table as he passed it. He was hungry.

Bunn suddenly laughed out loud. *I own a bar and grill, and I come home hungry! Not too good for publicity, Bunn ole boy!*

He rummaged through the cabinets trying to find something that appealed to him. Finally, he settled on a bowl of Raisin Bran. At least it wasn't fried or grilled, and it had no smell. He sat down on the sofa, placed the bowl of cereal on the coffee table, and poured a generous amount of milk over it. Grabbing the remote, he pressed the power button. You could get some pretty good old movies at three o'clock in the morning. Tonight, a John Wayne western was on.

However, as Bunn ate his bowl of Raisin Bran, his mind wasn't on the old western movie. He stared at the invitation, then picked it up again.

Wonder who is getting this shebang together? he thought. Then he read on down the page.

Betty Hartford Hill. Betty Hartford...Betty Hartford? The name sounds familiar, but I can't put a face to it. She must still live in Masonville.

Bunn laid the invitation back on the coffee table to finish his Raisin

Bran, then lit a cigarette. He could always think better with a cigarette in his hand.

Betty Hartford. He leaned back on the sofa and blew a ring of smoke. Slowly his eyes took on a knowing look. *Yeah, Betty Hartford! She was the little poor girl from out in the Bush Creek section of town. Her father was a handyman of some sort. Yeah! She was poor, but she had a snotty attitude: like it was everybody else's fault she was poor. Wow! She must have done well, or she wouldn't want to be getting together with old classmates. Maybe I'll Google her later and see what I can find out. Oh well, it doesn't matter. I'm not going to the stupid reunion anyway.*

Bunn dozed off watching the movie and thinking about his high school years.

And he's going...and he's going...and it's a touchdown! It's a touchdown for Bunn Morris! That boy can move!

Bunn jumped as he awakened from the dream, papers flying as he kicked the coffee table. He had been back in his hometown, hightailing it down the football field for another six points, just like he had done so many times in high school. The fans and his teammates were cheering loudly for him.

"Bunn, Bunn, he's our man! If he can't do it, nobody can!"

"Go Bunn! Go Bunn! Go all the way!"

Those were the days! He had it all! Then suddenly, he had nothing.

When did it all seem to go wrong? He asked himself. *One minute I was a football, baseball, and basketball star, and the next I was nothing but a wreck.*

He lit a cigarette as his mother's face appeared in his mind. *That's when life changed,* his heart proclaimed.

He nodded as if someone was there to see the nod, remembering that horrible night. His father had never had time for his oldest son, but his mother was everything to him: his encourager, his conscience, his fan. She was always there for him, and she'd never missed one of his games until...

She was diagnosed with ovarian cancer. The doctors said nothing could be done, and gave her two to three months. He had just a few months left with the most important person in his world. A tear slid from Bunn's eye, and he let it find its way down his plump ruddy face, dropping to his wrinkled shirt. She had suffered so. He could still hear the moaning from her bedroom, although when he went to check on her or say goodnight, she held back the moans and smiled through the obvious pain. Sometimes, she had just had her pain medicine and was able to talk to him like the mother he had always known.

"Bunn, I want you to know I'm proud of you, and I want you to make something of your life. You have so much potential."

Taking her hand, Bunn replied, "You'll be right here to keep me straight, Mom."

"No, Bunn. I'm not going to be here much longer. I'm afraid I won't get to see you graduate."

Bunn wiped a tear, dispelling his attempt at bravery. "Now, Mom, don't talk like that. You are going to get well."

She shook her head. "I need you to be strong, my darling boy. I can face this better knowing you can handle it. You need to be strong for your dad and your brother; neither of them have your strength. Bunn, I want you to go to college and make something of yourself. I know you'll get a football scholarship. Make the most of your life, son. Make your mother proud."

He'd promised her he would, but he had let her down. The most important person in his life, and he had let her down. She would be so disappointed in him.

Bunn's dad never seemed to grasp the situation, or didn't want to. His response to the discovery that his wife had cancer was to stay away as much as possible. He came home late every night and went straight to the separate bedroom far down the hall, where he slept after the diagnosis so that he wouldn't have to hear her moans of pain. Bunn didn't know where he went every night before finally coming home, but suspected his father was drinking heavily—and possibly finding solace in other women. He had never been there for Bunn in the good times, and he definitely wasn't there during the bad. Bunn's spoiled younger brother Dave ran with a crowd Bunn wanted nothing to do with. They were into some bad stuff, and he knew it was only a matter of time until Dave got into trouble. All Bunn had was his mother, and now he was going to lose her.

She died two months before he graduated as he sat alone by her bedside. That's when Bunn stopped caring about anything. That's when he stopped believing in God; how could a so-called loving God let this happen? Oh, he went on to college for less than a year. He knew that when he left Masonville his life would change; he just hadn't known how drastic the change would be. The athletic scholarship guaranteed him a free ride as long as he did his part, but Bunn's heart just wasn't in it. He missed his mother and hated his father, and that hate just ate away at him. Oddly, he had no feelings at all for his brother. One semester was all he lasted in football, and he flunked almost every course. What was the use? Bunn didn't care anymore. When he flunked out, he didn't go back home. The day he left Masonville for college, he had simply loaded his car and drove away with no good-byes. He had nothing to say to his father or his brother. He packed his bags once more when leaving college, this time heading for eastern Virginia where he was going to make it BIG! He made it big, all right. Many nights he slept in alleys with the homeless, not willing to admit he was one of them. Then he got in with a group of hippies, and he didn't even want to remember what that was like. Most of the time he was so strung out on weed, booze, and the harder stuff he didn't even know where he was.

Two years after his mother's death, he ran into someone from Masonville—couldn't even remember who it was—who told him his dad and brother had moved away. Dave had gotten into some trouble (no surprise there), and his father had decided they needed a new beginning.

Guess I needed a new beginning, too, thought Bunn, with a dry laugh. *This ole boy didn't make it in big time football, and he hasn't made it so far in the real world. That's for certain.* He roughly stubbed out his cigarette in an already full ash tray, releasing his anger. *Most Athletic...huh!*

Then one day, Bunn had stumbled into a soup kitchen, ragged, dirty, and half starved. That's where he'd met Pastor Bob. Bunn smelled the wonderful aroma of food as he opened the door, but he was so weak he just barely made it to a table before he collapsed. The next thing he knew, a man was shaking him and handing him a cup of coffee. Bunn had to have help to lift the cup to his mouth.

"I'm here to help you, son. Just take it nice and easy. God has led you to the right place."

Bunn remembered thinking, *God don't even know me. Why would he lead me here?*

Another man brought him a bowl of soup and placed it in front of him, and the first man even helped him feed himself.

"They call me Pastor Bob, son," he said, in the kindest voice Bunn had ever heard. "I'm here to help you. You don't need to be afraid, because you've come to a place where you can get back on the right path. God loves you, whether you know it or not, and I love you, too. Now eat the rest of that soup slowly, then I'll take you to a room where you can sleep. When you wake up, we'll get you cleaned up and get some more food in you."

Bunn remembered the last thought he'd had before falling asleep: *God loves you, son.*

The next morning when he awoke, he had no idea where he was or how he had ended up there, but he could smell *food*; he thought it was the most pleasant smell in the world. Looking around, he saw he was in a small room with soft, clean colors and in a bed with clean sheets. It had been a long time since he had slept in a bed. It was warm, too; oh, it was so warm.

There was a knock at the door, and then it opened slowly. Bunn remembered the face.

"Good morning. You probably don't remember much about last night, but I'm Pastor Bob. Are you ready to get cleaned up and have a good warm meal?"

"Yes...yes, sir," he replied. "I guess I am."

Soon Bunn was the cleanest he had been in months, with clean clothes. They looked to be second hand, but that didn't matter. They were clean and they fit. His hair was even clean.

"Boy, you look almost human," laughed Pastor Bob. "Now let's get you fed. Pick you up a tray and go through the line. They'll fill it for you, and if you need seconds, just go back and get it. When you're full, we'll talk a bit."

That was the beginning of a new life for Bunn. He stayed at the shelter for two months; in that time, he was treated with the only love he had ever known, except his mother's. He had three good meals a day, a room to sleep in, and clean clothes to wear. Each day he had chores to do to earn his keep, and each day he attended two classes: one a Bible study, and the other a class to help him deal with the outside world. There were several men in the class, as this was a shelter for men only. At the end of two months, Pastor

Bob had helped him find a job. It wasn't anything big, but it was a start. He was cleanup man in a small restaurant, and it included a small room in the back. Two evenings a week, Bunn went back to the shelter to help out and to attend the two classes. He even attended Pastor Bob's little church on the Sundays when he didn't have to work. He and God were not exactly friends yet, but they were getting there.

Then he met Marla. She wasn't a hippie, but neither was she into spiritual things. She was a waitress in another little café, about six blocks from the shelter. He went there for coffee and a change of scenery now and then, when he had a little extra money. They started talking each time. Marla was a petite little redhead full of spunk, not beautiful but not bad to look at, and she had a contagious sense of humor. She convinced her boss to hire Bunn to do whatever jobs needed doing. She took him to her apartment, made him a bed on her couch, and saw to it that he had three decent meals a day. After a few months, he moved up to a cook in the café and finally part-time manager. Before the year was out, he and Marla married. Big mistake! They hadn't talked about what they wanted from the marriage; when he found out she wanted the cozy little cottage and kids, he took off.

That's when Bunn headed for Chicago, and a few months later he received divorce papers from Marla, along with a note telling him she was pregnant.

"I don't expect anything from you," she said. "I just thought you should know."

Seven months later, he received the last note from her. The baby was a girl, but she didn't even give him a name...and Marla was getting married again. That was forty-some years ago, and Bunn had never heard from her again. For all he knew, he was probably a grandpa.

In Chicago, Bunn messed around with a few jobs and then went to work for Mr. Joseph P. Tanner, proprietor of a bar and grill. Ole J.P. was a drinking, cussing, laughing, storytelling, beanpole of a man, but he took to Bunn right off. He gave him an apartment up over the bar and grill free of charge, asking that Bunn keep an eye on the business during closed hours.

Bunn stared at the ceiling. *The same magnificent apartment I live in today.* He laughed. *Mom would be so proud of me. Oh, and Mr. Banning, my dear high school principal, I bet he would just be singing my praises all over Masonville High.*

Bunn Morris, the success story!

Bunn had moved up in the bar and grill working for J.P. Tanner, partly because he worked hard and partly because the old man took a liking to him. By the time he had been there five years, he was running the place. Tanner was getting up in years. One day, he'd called Bunn into his office.

"Bunn, I'm going to be short and to the point here. I've been diagnosed with liver cancer. I think we can both guess why. A man's lifestyle just catches up with him sooner or later. Doc says I don't have long: maybe just a few weeks. I'm telling you this because I want to sell you the grill."

Bunn had grown pale as J.P. talked, and his heart was racing. One more person he cared about was dying from cancer.

"Are you sure, J.P.?" he asked.

"Wouldn't be telling you if I wasn't, boy. I have to make some plans. I have a daughter who lives in Arizona. We haven't kept in touch since her mama died; didn't keep in touch much even before that, really. She never cared for me and the life I've lived—and I can't say as I blame her, since I was never a father to her. I would like to leave her a little money, though. It won't make up for being a lousy father, but it would allow me to die a little easier."

"I don't know if I can afford to buy the grill, J.P.," Bunn said. "I have saved some money over the years, but I don't know that it's enough. What are you asking?"

"Oh, not much, son. I just want a little for Gloria, and I would die a little happier knowing you were taking over this place. It ain't much, but it's been the only family I've had in many years and you're a part of this place. I don't want to get all mushy here, but Bunn, you're like a son to me."

This really choked Bunn up. "Sir, you are more like a father to me than my real father ever was. You gave me a chance and trusted me and believed in me. What would you have to have for the place?"

"How does twenty thousand sound to you, boy?"

Bunn's eyes flew open and he almost toppled out of his chair.

"Twenty thousand? Why, J.P., it's worth ten times that! Even more!"

"Bunn, boy, I can't take it with me, and I want someone to have it that cares about it. I just want some money to leave my daughter. I have enough already to pay my bills and the funeral expenses. Those are already taken care of. Now, do we have a deal?"

Bunn rose and reached out his hand to Mr. Tanner. "Yes, sir. We most definitely have a deal. Thank you, sir."

They shook hands and then J.P. threw his arms around Bunn and pulled him into a hug. The next day they filled out the necessary papers, and within a week the bar and grill belonged to Bunn. J.P. mailed a check to his estranged daughter. Two weeks later, he died. His daughter cashed her check, but never wrote to her father.

After a restless night, Bunn arose around five a.m., ate a stale doughnut with coffee, and got ready for another day of the same routine. J.P. had done well by him, and he had tried to do well by J.P. by making a real go of the business. Customers seemed to like the place, because they kept coming back. He wasn't rich, but he definitely made a good living.

Bunn put on the first pot of coffee when he came downstairs and began filling the napkin holders. The cooks, Ray and Gid, usually showed up about seven to get things going, and Marsha came in around seven-thirty. The three had been with him a long time, and were about as dependable as workers could ever be. Ray had come looking for a job one day, fresh out of prison. Bunn liked him right off and decided to give him a chance. Neither had ever been sorry. Gid had been into drugs and came to the grill after going through a rehabilitation program. He now had a wife and son, and he wanted to give them a decent life. Marsha was single, in her middle years, and supported her aging mother. She liked to boss Bunn around sometimes, concerning his life, but he didn't really mind. The three of them were the only semblance of a family he had. The other young waitress, Sally, had only been with them about six months, but she did her job well, was always on time, and never asked for time off. She had a little one to support on her own, and she was thankful for the work. The other waitresses were part-time workers, and they came and went as often as you would change bed linens.

Bunn never opened the grill before nine each morning, and closed at eleven each night. It made for some long hours, but he had to do what it took to make a decent living. His life hadn't turned out the way he had planned, but it wasn't such a bad life.

The front door opened and Ray and Gid came in, bringing a draft of wind with them. That's the one thing Bunn hated most about Chicago...that confounded wind.

"Morning, boss," called Ray. "It's so blustery out there today a man does well to keep his pants on."

"Maybe that will drive customers in here for some warm food and coffee," responded Bunn.

The guys said no more, but set in to making biscuits, getting out the fixings for gravy, and setting out a few dozen eggs. Another gust of wind a few minutes later brought Marsha in.

"Whoo-eee! I'm glad I don't wear a wig!"

"And I thought all these years you did," said Bunn, an innocent look masking his humor.

"Don't you get on my bad side today, boss," she warned. "I'll put some strychnine in your coffee."

Bunn laughed. "Now, Marsha, you know you couldn't live without me."

She chose to ignore that and went about her work preparations. She usually tidied up whatever needed it, then helped Ray and Gid until opening time. They always worked as a team.

"Whatcha looking at there, boss?" she asked, as she brought Bunn a fresh cup of coffee.

"Nothing," he replied, pulling the paper over toward him. That didn't save him, though. Marsha snatched the paper and began to read aloud.

"You are cordially invited to our Fifty-Year Class Reunion at Masonville High School—" Bunn snatched the paper back.

"Fifty-year reunion! Whew, diddly! Bunn, you are an old man. Did you hear that, boys? Our Bunny Boy is going to his fifty-year high school reunion. We better be buying this old guy a cane and some of them one-a-day vitamins."

Bunn tried to conceal his flaming face, but it was useless—and Marsha was enjoying every second of it.

"Who said I was going?" he countered, wadding the paper and putting it in his pocket.

"Not going? Why, of course you're going. You can't miss your fifty-year reunion. You might not live 'til the next one! How many others did you go to?"

"As far as I know, this is the first they've ever had," he answered, picking up his newspaper to close the subject.

"The first? Wow! Well, you've got to go. Can you imagine what those people look like now, and what they've done in their lives? This could be *very* interesting!"

"A whole lot more than I've done with mine," he replied, "and I certainly hope they look better."

"Bunn Morris," Marsha said in her motherly voice, hands on hips, "you've done quite well for yourself. You own your own little café, and you make a good living. Now, what's not to be proud of in that?"

"Time to open up," said Bunn, rising from his chair and heading for the door. As far as he was concerned, the conversation was over. Knowing Marsha, however, this would not be the end of it. When she got something in her craw, she held on to it like a hen on a June bug.

The wolves were circling, coming closer and closer until she could smell their hot, fetid breath. Guttural, menacing growls came from their mouths, their horrible fangs exposed, and their eyes reflected the fire of the pits of hell. Closer and closer they came, until she thought she would suffocate. Then there was only one and it was not the head of a wolf, but that of a man with fangs and fiery eyes. The guttural sounds still issued forth, as did the fetid breath, and as she lay gasping and retching, his face became the face of the devil himself.

Audra awoke suddenly, drenched in perspiration and shaking in fear. She looked around the room, searching for this creature that could be nothing less than the devil. When she was sure he was not there, she got out of bed and stumbled to the bathroom to wash her face in cold water. She stood for a moment looking into the bathroom mirror at a deathly pale face she hardly recognized. It had been a long time since she had had this dream: years, in fact. After another swish of her face with the cold water, she made her way to the kitchen, turned on the light, and poured herself a glass of water. She needed the lights on, so she turned on the living room light, too. Audra sat on the plush white sofa, tightly hugging her knees, not daring to go back to bed. What had caused this dream all of a sudden? Then, as if drawn by a force, her eyes focused on the invitation to her class reunion.

"You are the cause of this," she said, as if the invitation had ears. "You brought back memories I've tried so hard to rid myself of. It's your fault."

The school didn't cause your problems, a voice in her mind seemed to say. *It was your only escape from the darkness and evil. It was your refuge, and your class-mates were your only friends.*

Unable to stand the silence any longer, she walked to her stereo and pushed the button. Immediately the song began to play. "You've lost that lovin' feelin'..." Audra tried to reach out and turn it off, but her hand wouldn't move. The song from her high school days continued to play, and the memories came...

"Audra, you must sit like a lady at all times," said her mother. "Your father is a preacher of God's word, and we must never bring any condemnation on him."

Audra didn't know what *condemnation* was, but she pulled her dress down just a little more and pressed her knees tight together.

"Audra, you most certainly cannot wear shorts."

"But why, mother?"

"Audra, your father is a preacher, and shorts are of the devil. Bad girls wear things like that. Do you want your father to be displeased with you? I think you know what his displeasure brings. Do you want God to be displeased with you? Do you want to feel God's wrath? Or your father's?"

Audra definitely didn't want that. She knew all too well what happened when her father was displeased. She knew all about his wrath. Red streaks still marked the back of her legs from other times she had displeased him. Once, when a visiting preacher and his wife came to dinner, she had decided to entertain them (and herself) by doing cartwheels, like she had seen the cheerleaders do at school pep rallies. She had been practicing when no one was around, but she forgot what happens when you turn a cartwheel with a dress on.

The preacher's wife had gasped, putting a starched white handkerchief to her mouth. Her father roared, "Audra, stop that!"

She immediately knew she had done something that brought condemnation on her father, and she tried to look remorseful—but mostly she just looked scared.

Audra's father grabbed her roughly by the arm, his fingers biting into her skin unmercifully.

"Apologize *immediately* to these dear, Godly people!" he roared.

"I-I-I'm sorry," she stammered, with what little strength she had left.

"Louder!" her father roared again.

"I'm *sorry!*"

"Now, you go to your room. There will be no supper for you tonight."

Audra walked as fast as she could to her room and threw herself onto her bed, knowing from experience that her punishment was not over. Before closing her bedroom door, she heard the visiting preacher say, "The devil is always lurking, Brother James, crouching and tempting our children. We must administer strong punishment, or he will quickly take over. *Strong* punishment, Brother James. Our children must not shame us."

It must have been two hours later when she heard the preacher and his wife say good night. Then she heard her parents talking, their words muted. The talking ceased and the door to her room opened, creaking ominously as they both walked in. Her father held the leather strop in his hand, and she could see the anger in his eyes.

"Girl, you shamed me in front of a man of God and his wife. You have the devil in you, and it is my job to get him out."

She looked to her mother for help, but there was no pity there. What Audra saw was almost a sneer on her mother's face, as though she found pleasure in what was about to happen.

"Take off your underpants, Audra," she said.

Audra slowly obeyed.

"Now, bend over the bed. Your father must do his duty."

"You shamed me, girl," said her father again, "and when you shame me, you shame God. The devil is in you, and I must drive him from this house!"

Her father's voice boomed even louder, "Be *gone*, Satan!"

With this, he brought the leather strop down on her backside with full force. Audra gritted her teeth and clenched her fists, determined not to cry.

"Get thee out of my house!" he roared again, bringing the strop down even harder the second time.

"I will not let you offend me!" he shouted, and once more the strop came down, tearing her flesh.

Audra didn't know how many times the leather strop did its duty, for she passed out after a few more. She woke up sore the next morning, and the covers stuck to her blood-coated skin. She winced as she pulled them gingerly away from her body. She must have wet the bed at some point; she could smell the urine. She needed to use the bathroom now, and it was all she could do not to cry out as she walked to the door of her bedroom, hoping no one was there to see her. The living room was empty, so she walked quietly on to the bathroom. She cried out as she sat on the commode, then quickly put her hand over her mouth, expecting any minute to feel the strop again.

When she walked back to her bedroom, her mother stood in the doorway with her arms crossed, eyes bright with triumph.

"I hope the punishment was sufficient to help you see the error of your ways," she said, a smirk on her face.

"Yes, ma'am," answered Audra, head bowed in remorse.

"You will not go to school today. You will stay home, wash those sheets, clean your entire room, and repent for your wicked ways."

Audra kept her head bowed but she knew why she was staying home today. Her mother didn't want people to see the welts and broken skin and perhaps ask questions. It was Friday, so they would have three days to heal.

"The shame you caused your father cannot be erased, but you will fast this day as you pray for God's forgiveness," continued her mother. "You are a wanton girl, trying to show your body parts to men. I know you were trying to tempt Brother Gibson and humiliate your father."

Audra didn't know what *wanton* meant, but she knew what hunger pains were, and right now her stomach was crying out for food.

"But I'm hungry, Mama."

"Hunger and fasting will help you to see the error of your ways," her mother replied, satisfaction in her voice. "By tomorrow you will understand what punishment is like for those who entertain the devil."

Audra went obediently to her room, for she knew what would happen if she disobeyed. Her mother never punished her physically, but saw to it that her father did. She felt only hate and disappointment exuding from her mother, and she couldn't figure out what she had done to cause those feelings. The rest of the day was spent washing sheets and cleaning her room, then Bible reading and prayer.

I hate reading this Bible, Audra had thought, frowning. *It talks about Jesus and love, and I don't see any of that in my father. He's supposed to be a man of God, but he hates everything and everybody. Everything is sinful to him, and everybody is a sinner. He never mentions anything about love when he preaches. He says I was born evil, but I don't understand that. I try to be good. If God is anything like my father, I don't want to know him.*

Audra withdrew from the memories, hearing the song playing again.

"You've lost that lovin' feeling... Now it's gone, gone, gone oh, oh, oh..."

"I never had any loving feelings to lose, and no one ever showed me any love."

Audra caught a quick breath as she realized she had spoken the words aloud. Then she smiled sadly. The only love she'd ever felt was from a boy she once knew from her class, a boy from Masonville High.

"I wonder what happened to him?" she asked, but only the walls heard the question.

"Oh, Harm!" squealed Rosalee. "A class reunion! I can't wait to meet your high school friends!"

Harmon Cline had just shown his wife the invitation to his fifty-year class reunion, thinking she would laugh at the idea. Big mistake! She had laughed, all right, but not in the way he had imagined. That woman could still get excited over things like a child, and she was definitely excited over his class reunion.

"I have no interest in going back to a place I haven't seen in fifty years," he said. "I can't even remember most of those people, and I'm quite sure I won't recognize them at this age. Can you imagine how everyone has changed from eighteen to sixty-eight? I'm sure everyone hasn't remained as young and good looking as yours truly."

Rosalee planted a kiss on his cheek. "That's right! If they look as good as my Harmie, they should be thankful."

They sat down to eat, and no more was said about the invitation. While Rosalee did the dishes, Harm went over some paperwork. Then they sat down to watch television together for awhile. By ten, they were ready for bed.

Sleep did not come easy for Harm, however. His mind wandered back to those high school years. Truth be told, he had enjoyed a lot of it, especially the sports: basketball, baseball, and even football. Sports and his teammates were his escape—not that his home life was so bad. He had a wonderful mother, but she was so busy taking care of a kid and trying to make a living that she had little time for talks and doing things together like most families. Then there was the stigma of not having a father. He could see the mocking look on people's faces. *Illegitimate!* Lord, how he hated that word. Of course, it was better than the *other* word they used. His mother never knew he found out the identity of his father by snooping into her private things.

"Some things you are just better off not knowing, Harm," she would say.

"But, Mom, don't you think I deserve to know?"

"Deserving and needing are two different things."

Harm had no idea what the heck that meant, but he let the matter drop... at least for a time.

After graduation, Harm joined the Army. It was really his only choice. There was no money for college, and no job where he could really make a good living. Six months after enlisting, he was sent to Vietnam. He didn't know what to expect, but nothing could have prepared him for that place.

Lord, what an awful place that was...the heat, the hunger, the fighting, the fear, the dying.

The memories came flooding back.

The noise of the guns, grenades, and explosions was deafening. Those Viet Cong could think up more booby traps and more ways to kill a man than he could ever have imagined. They weren't even human. Men were dropping everywhere; some were blown into pieces that went flying in all directions. Most of the soldiers were young men, still in their teens even.

They didn't know anything about fighting. It was hard to even know who the enemy was. They all looked alike, and the danger was everywhere. His best buddy, Thacker, had been one of the unlucky ones. Just twenty years old, he would never go back home to his wife and unborn child. Tears swam down Harm's face as he tried to stop the memories. He finally got up and went to the kitchen for a glass of water. He wiped the tears from his face and threw cold water on it, but the memories just wouldn't stop.

Think about something good, Harm. Think about something good.

Hearing the little voice of reason inside of him, Harm tried to reroute his thoughts. He thought of Rosalee. He remembered getting off the bus that had carried him from Texas to Michigan. He hadn't known anything about Michigan, but one of his buddies had told him it was a good place to get a job.

As he left the bus, there was a group of hippies standing nearby, flowers in their hair and leis around their neck. The paraphernalia couldn't hide the dirt, though. It was apparent they weren't too fond of baths. They were looking at him and saying the nastiest things, disgust written plainly on their faces.

"There's one more baby killer," called one, just loud enough for Harm to hear.

"Bet he feels proud of himself, fighting people he don't even know anything about!"

Two of the half-naked women with flowers in their hair walked toward Harm and spat at him. Luckily, they missed their target.

Then, all of a sudden, he saw the most beautiful sight he had ever seen in his life. A young girl walked toward him. She had long black hair and the most radiant skin he had ever beheld, not to mention a flawless figure. In her hand she carried a red rose. When she was within a couple of feet of him, she reached out and handed the rose to him.

Harm stood there speechless.

"Thank you for serving our country," she said. "My name is Rosalee Slade."

The hippies were soon forgotten. He was lost in her soft brown eyes.

"Hello to you, Rosalee Slade," he said, with the first smile his face had shown in months.

"I'm sorry about those stupid people," she said. "Don't let them spoil your return. How about if I take you to dinner?"

Harm laughed aloud. "You don't even know me, Rosalee Slade. Why would you want to take me to dinner?"

She smiled, and her eyes lit up. "Because you have just returned from what I suspect has been a horrifying experience, and I think you deserve a good meal and a friend. So, what do you say?"

Harm smiled as he was swallowed by those beautiful eyes. "I would love to go to dinner with you, Rosalee Slade."

"I think just Rosalee will do," she said, linking her arm through his and leading him from the bus station. The hippies were still shouting out their taunts, but he was lost in the eyes of the girl on his arm.

It was one of the best nights of Harm's life. They ate at a small, quiet restaurant called Bennie's Grill, and he had the most delicious meal he had eaten in two years. They talked and laughed, and for awhile, Vietnam was forgotten. They saw each other almost every day after that, and two weeks later she took him home to meet her dad. Her mother had died three years before. Harm hit it off with her dad immediately, and Mr. Slade offered him a job at his trucking firm. That was the beginning of a new life.

Finally settling down from his flashbacks, Harm took another drink of water, washed his face one more time, and returned to bed. He turned to look at Rosalee.

Yes, she's the best thing that ever happened to me.

Harm's mind was made up. He would not be going back to Masonville. There was nothing there for him; all he needed or wanted was lying right beside him.

Sybil pulled the mask away from her eyes to look at the bedside clock.

Ten o'clock.

She pulled the mask back over her eyes and turned over. She and Arthur had gotten home late, or maybe early, from the Hemming's party. It must have been three a.m., which was not unusual, but in the last few years it seemed more difficult to be out so late. Arthur seemed to thrive on it, and Sybil had to admit that their age difference was beginning to show in more ways than one. There was a big difference in 56 and 68. Maybe Arthur was noticing it, too. She saw how he had looked at some of the younger women. He had strayed several times during their marriage, but she had never felt it had anything to do with age...until now. Maybe she was blaming age because she suddenly just felt old. Maybe it was that darn class reunion invitation. As hard as she had tried, she couldn't get it out of her mind. Something seemed to be pulling her.

Why would you want to go back there, girl? There was never anything good for you there. You have no friends there.

There is Charlie...

The name seemed to come from out of the blue. No one knew about Charlie, and she didn't want to think about him. He was another dark part of her past. Her heart hurt when she thought about Charlie.

"Sybil, are you going to sleep all day?"

Arthur's voice interrupted her thoughts. She lifted the mask once more to see him standing in the bedroom doorway, dressed and handsome in a white polo shirt and green golf slacks. He must be planning to head to the green.

"I'm getting up. Didn't realize it was so late. That was quite a party last night."

"Yeah, the Hemmings really know how to throw a bash. I really enjoyed it. What are you going to do today?"

"I thought I'd go down to the salon and check things out, just make sure everything is running smoothly. Then I'm supposed to have a late lunch with Sarah Bradley and Mary Amos. I'm sure they'll want to gossip about the party."

Arthur came to her bedside, gave her a perfunctory kiss and turned to leave.

"Arthur," said Sybil, "could we talk just a moment?"

She patted the bed beside her and after a slight hesitation, he sat.

"Is something wrong, Syb?"

She looked at him for a moment, trying to find the words she wanted. "Arthur, how would you feel about going to a class reunion?"

He looked at her strangely. "A class reunion? What kind of a class reunion?"

"My high school class of sixty-five is having a reunion in June...the first ever. It's been fifty years. At first, I thought, *No way!* But the more I've thought about it, the more I think it might be a good idea."

Arthur studied her for a moment. "This seems important to you, Syb. What makes it so important?"

"There's a lot you don't know about me, Arthur. There are things I've never told you because it was just too hard to talk about."

"I'm listening now."

He reached over and took her hand, and Sybil saw true concern in his eyes.

"Arthur, I grew up poor. Not just a little poor, but *dirt* poor. My father was lazy, and a gambler...just a no-good bum. What clothes I had were either secondhand or homemade. The other kids taunted me and made fun of me."

Raising her up in bed, Arthur held her to his chest.

"My sweet Sybil. I had no idea. Let's go to that reunion so I can punch all of them in the nose!"

Sybil laughed in spite of her sadness.

"I think it might do me good to go back. I want them to know I have made something of myself, and I want them to see my handsome husband. Maybe all of that shouldn't be important, but it is. I guess, also, I just need to face my ghosts. They have had control of me for too long."

"Then it's settled. We will go."

"Arthur...there's something else."

She reached over to the dresser drawer and pulled out the letter from her father. Without words, she handed it to her husband and he opened it and read. Then he just looked at her.

"How long has this money business been going on?"

"For years. I'm afraid if I don't send it to him, he might come here and embarrass me."

"Sybil, why haven't you told me about this? I'm your husband."

"I was just so ashamed."

"Well, your days of worrying about this are over. I will handle it."

"What will you do?"

"Do you trust me?"

"Of course, Arthur."

"Then, no questions. I will handle it, and in a legal way. You might say I will put the fear of God into the old cuss. Thank you for finally sharing this with me, my love. Now, you just get prepared for that high school reunion. We're going to wow those people!"

Arthur patted her hand and left. Sybil had never felt so loved and so at peace in all her life. Yes, she would definitely be happy to show Arthur off to her classmates, but not for the original reasons.

"Hey, Baker! Let's step it up there!"

Willie simply nodded and tried to work a little faster. His boss stayed on him a lot. He didn't know if he just liked to throw his weight around, or if he was trying to rile Willie and cause trouble with his parole officer. Willie would not let that happen. Whatever it took, he was not going back to that place. It wasn't as bad as 'Nam, but it was pretty awful. At least in 'Nam he wasn't confined to four walls. Well, sometimes he was confined to four very tight walls, but he didn't want to think about that. Nope, he would not go back. He hadn't been much of a success, but he could improve what life he had left.

Someone dropped a crate and Willie crouched, his heart racing, waiting for the sound of gunfire or an explosion. The men around stopped and stared, then began to laugh.

"What's wrong there, Baker? Someone shooting at you?"

Willie ignored them as he stood up and continued on with his work. Later, one of the men sauntered over to him. Looking back over his shoulder to make sure no one was in listening range, he said quietly, "You were in Vietnam, weren't you, Baker?"

Turning away, Willie answered, "What of it?"

"One Vet can always tell another," said the man.

Willie stopped and turned back to look at him. "You a 'Nam vet?"

"Yes, in sixty-eight. Spent two years in that hell hole. It's something you just never get over. Saw friends killed, other soldiers blown to pieces, and men with limbs blown off so they wished they had been killed. And what was it all for? We came home hated by everyone. Yeah, I know what it's like to dive for cover at loud sounds, but those who stayed here and led soft lives or hauled off to Canada don't have a clue. They think it's funny, but I never saw anything over there to laugh about."

Willie stared into space. "Yeah, you go over there thinking you're doing the right thing by serving your country, and you come home to hate and disgust, with crowds of lily-livered idiots doped up and wearing flowers, protesting the war and calling us war mongers and baby killers. It's like we were the bad guys."

They stood quietly for a moment, each lost in his own haunted memories. Then the man reached out his hand.

"I'm Bear Branson," he said. "Well, it's really *Bartholomew*, but who wants to be called a name like that? In 'Nam, they called me Bear."

"Willie Baker," replied Willie, shaking Bear's hand. "My folks named me Wilson, but who wants to be called a name like that?"

Both laughed and the atmosphere seemed much lighter.

"I was in Nam in sixty-six and sixty-seven," volunteered Willie. "Tunnel rat most of the time."

Bear's face took on a new respect. "You were a tunnel rat? Lord, man, you have really been through it! Guess that makes for some real nightmares. Wasn't no worse job over there."

"Yeah, kinda gets to you after a while," said Willie, again getting that faraway look.

"Hey, man, how about we go out for a bite after work today?" Bear suggested.

Willie considered the invitation for a moment. He hadn't really made any friends since he got out of jail, but it might be nice to have some conversation for a change.

He nodded. "OK, but I'm pretty strapped until payday. It'll have to be somewhere dirt cheap."

"Tell you want," said Bear. "I'm a pretty fair cook. Why don't we just eat over at my place? It'll be quiet, and we won't have to watch for 'Congs around every corner."

After the whistle blew that evening, Bear and Willie headed for Bear's place. It wasn't much to look at, but it was clean—and it was nicer than Willie's dump. True to his word, Bear cooked up a good meal of spaghetti, salad, and breadsticks taken from the freezer and baked just right. It was the best meal Willie had eaten in a year. After they finished, Bear washed the dishes and Willie dried. Then they headed to the couch to relax.

"So," began Bear, "are you married, Willie?"

"No," replied Willie, emphatically shaking his head. "That's just not in the cards for me. I have nothing to offer a woman except poverty and nightmares. How about you?"

"Oh, I tried it a couple of times," said Bear, his voice taking on a sadness. "Once when I was just back from 'Nam. Nell was a pretty little thing, and for awhile we had a good thing going, but it soon got old to her. She liked to go out dancing, and I wasn't much for crowds. She said I was making an old woman out of her, so she left and I soon got divorce papers. I stayed single for about twenty years after that, and then I met Mona. She was a waitress at a little café where I use to eat dinner pretty often. We got to talking, then we started going out. After a year or so, we tied the knot. Shouldn't have done it, and it didn't last long. She wanted me to let her two grown children live with us and mooch off of me. When I said an emphatic 'No,' she said an emphatic 'So long!' After that, I decided I was better off living the single life. Now, what's your story? Surely there's been a woman in your life somewhere along the way."

Willie sat quietly for a moment. "I guess the only woman I ever felt anything for was a pretty little girl in high school. Her name was Audra, and she was one *beautiful* girl."

"What happened?"

"Nothing really. That was the problem. We walked to classes together and talked when we could, but her father was an old-time preacher man; he wouldn't let her date at all. Scariest man I ever knew, and Audra was scared to death of him. After graduation I left Masonville and I lost track of her. If she got away from her old man, she's probably married with six kids and umpteen grand kids. Nope, there's no one for old Willie."

Bear laughed. "It may be fifty years in the past, man, but from the look I see in your eyes when you say her name, I think you've still got a thing for her."

"You know, it's strange we are talking about this," said Willie. "I just got an invitation the other day to my high school class' fifty-year reunion. Fifty years! Can you imagine that?"

"It might just be your opportunity," said Bear. "You oughta go, man. Get it out of your system once and for all. She may have been pining away for you all these years, and you didn't even know it."

"Couldn't go if I wanted to," said Willie sadly.

"Why's that?"

Willie looked at Bear for a moment, trying to make a decision.

"There's something you don't know about me."

Bear just looked at Willie, allowing him to make his decision. Bear had been around long enough to recognize when a man was struggling with something.

"I've been in prison," blurted Willie before he could change his mind.

Bear smiled. "Half the men I know have been there at one time or another, especially vets. Things just get too much for us sometimes, and we end up doing something foolish. Spent a few nights in the pokey myself for being drunk and disorderly. Didn't like it much. How long were you in?"

"Eighteen months," replied Willie. "I'm still on parole. You haven't asked what I was in for."

"Figured if you wanted me to know, you'd tell me. I don't mess into another man's business."

"I was in for possession of drugs," said Willie. "I got messed up on them after I came back from 'Nam. I guess it was easier than dealing with the nightmares and the name-calling. Not that that was any excuse. The easy way out is not all it's cracked up to be. It started pretty soon after I came stateside. I would get clean, then I'd relapse, get clean again, and then another relapse. The last time I got caught. Maybe prison was a good thing, though. I've been clean now for two years: the eighteen months in jail, and the six months I've been out."

Bear nodded. "I played around with them myself for awhile, but then I met Nell. She gave me a reason to quit. Then when things got rough again, I just said no to the drugs. Of course, I had some help."

"What do you mean?" asked Willie.

Bear pondered for a moment and then spoke. "Willie, there's someone I want you to meet. Would you consider going to church with me Sunday morning?"

Willie's face turned beet red. "No thanks, Bear. I'm not into this religious stuff. Pardon me. I don't mean to offend you. It's just not for me."

Bear laughed. "You sound exactly like me thirty or forty years ago. This is not like your traditional church, Willie. I wouldn't steer you wrong. Just go with me one time, and if you don't feel you should be there, I'll never mention it again."

Willie sat quietly a few minutes. "Let me think on it. I'll let you know by Friday."

"Good enough," said Bear. "Now, how about a cup of coffee?"

Willie stayed on another hour, talking about work, baseball, and casual things, then headed back to his lonely apartment. He couldn't remember when he had felt more at peace, and he certainly couldn't remember enjoying conversation and companionship more. It was good to be with someone who understood and didn't ask a million dumb questions. The only thing that bothered him was Bear's invitation to church on Sunday. Of course, Bear wouldn't put any pressure on him, but for some reason Willie felt drawn to the idea. When he was back home his father had made him go to church, but that was just to look respectable in the community. Willie had never felt anything except resentment. Folks there were mostly a bunch of hypocrites, especially his father. He remembered Audra's preacher father. If that was an example of church and God, he didn't want any part of it, and yet something was drawing him to go with Bear.

That night the nightmares came...not of Vietnam this time, but of his home life back in school days.

"Boy, get out there and cut that wood! Lord, I don't know how you'll ever amount to anything! You ain't big enough to ever make a man, and you shore 'nough ain't going to build any muscles with your nose stuck in a book. Now get out there!" Willie flinched in his sleep as he felt his father's boot kick him in the side.

Ferrell Baker had been drinking ever since he came home from work, a routine for him for as long as Willie could remember. He'd come home, sit in his recliner, and drink. Ferrell had been a big football star when he was in high school, and he had never forgiven Willie for being such a small guy. The fact that Willie was great in basketball just wasn't enough for him.

"Basketball is for sissies, boy! Get some muscle on you!"

Willie always made excellent grades. He was chosen Most Likely to Succeed and was third on the honor roll of his graduating class, but this didn't impress his father at all. People in Masonville had no idea what Ferrell was really like. They respected him as manager of The First Bank of Masonville. To add to his respectability, his father faithfully attended church on Sunday morning and served on various committees. His walking sure didn't match his talking, though. He was an out-and-out hypocrite. Ferrell took out all of his frustrations on Willie, but for some reason he never laid a hand on Carolyn, Willie's younger sister. Willie was thankful for that, and he had always tried to stand in the way of abuse toward his mother. Why she didn't leave Ferrell, Willie would never know. It seemed her standing in the town was more important than her well-being, or that of her son. He had overheard conversations between his parents a few times, and it seemed that his father had other women in his life. It didn't surprise Willie; it just added to the contempt he had for the old man.

"You ain't worth nothin', boy! You're a little ole wimpy runt. I'm plumb ashamed to tell people you're my son!"

Willie awoke the next morning drained from the nightmare. He didn't even feel like eating, but had a cup of coffee and headed out to work. He couldn't be late, and after work he had a meeting with his parole officer.

"Hey, Willie!" Bear greeted him as he clocked in. "You look tired today. I didn't poison you with my cooking, did I?"

Willie smiled weakly. "Nah, the food was great. It was just one of those nights. Say, Bear, if the invitation still holds, I think I'll try church on Sunday.

It may just be this once, but something seems to be drawing me to go."

Bear slapped him on the back. "That's how it begins, my friend. I don't think you'll be sorry."

Sunday morning rolled around, and as Willie had a piece of toast and a cup of coffee, his stomach was in knots.

Why on earth did you get yourself into this? He asked himself. But he had agreed to go, and if he was nothing else, Willie was a man of his word.

The address Bear had given him was not far from his apartment, so Willie could easily walk. As he rounded the corner and found the street number, Willie was confused. The place sure didn't look like a church. It looked like an old store building, maybe a restaurant. He was about ready to walk on when he heard Bear call his name.

"I see you made it!"

"Yeah, I wasn't sure this was the right place," said Willie. "Are you sure this is a church?"

Bear laughed. "I told you it was different. It don't have to have a steeple to be a church, you know. Come on in. I want you to meet Pastor Ben."

As they walked inside, Willie was more than a little curious. A man across the room saw them, smiled, and walked toward them.

"How ya doing, Bear?" he asked, shaking Bear's hand vigorously.

"Doing great," replied Bear. "Doing just great. I got somebody here I want you to meet. This is my friend Willie Baker. Willie, this is Pastor Ben."

Unable to help himself, Willie's mouth flew open. The man standing before him wore jeans and a t-shirt, not to mention the tattoos on his arms. His hair was short, however, and he was clean shaven.

Bear and Pastor Ben laughed.

"Don't be embarrassed," said Pastor Ben. "I get that reaction all the time. Bear was completely knocked off his feet when he first met me."

Willie finally calmed himself and shook hands with the pastor. "Sorry, sir, but I don't reckon I ever met a pastor that looks like you. Meaning no offense."

"No offense taken, Willie," he replied. "I have a story much like the stories of others in our little congregation. Unless I miss my guess, you are a vet. Right?"

"How can you tell?"

"I guess one vet just learns to recognize another."

Willie gaped once more. "You're a vet?"

"Yep. Vietnam, sixty-eight. Got a little memento from my time over there."He pulled up the left leg of his jeans to expose an artificial limb.

"When I came back from Nam, I was more dead than alive. As a matter of fact, at the time, it seemed that death would have been easier. I spent eight long months in a hospital. They had to amputate what leg I had left below the knee, and then I went through months of physical therapy and psych evaluation. Then I was fitted for this leg here and enjoyed more months of therapy. Needless to say, my attitude was not a good one."

"What changed?" asked Willie. "I mean, you sure seem to have a good attitude now, and I couldn't even detect a limp when you walked across the room."

Pastor Ben smiled and Willie noticed a certain glow about him.

"The only way I know to explain it," said Pastor Ben, "is that I met someone; his name was Jesus, and I've never been the same since. Each day is a new adventure for me. That's why I started this little church. I want others to meet the man I met. I want others to feel what I feel. Come on over and have some breakfast, and we'll get started with the service in a few minutes."

In the weeks following, Willie went to church every Sunday and every Thursday night. He just couldn't get enough of the things Pastor Ben talked about. A Jesus who died on a cross so all people could be saved if they chose to accept his gift. A God who loves us no matter what we have done, even a man named Paul who started out killing Christians. Willie thought of the men he had killed in 'Nam, even though it was in a war. It was hard to believe, but Willie believed, and two months later, Pastor Ben baptized him. Willie was happy for the first time in his life.

One Thursday night after the service, Pastor Ben took Willie aside.

"I hope you won't think we were talking behind your back, Willie, but Bear tells me your high school class is having a reunion. Have you thought about going?"

Willie nodded. "Yeah, I've thought about it. There's a lot I left unfinished back there: mostly feelings of hurt and even hate. I think it might do me good to go back, but I can't even if I do want to. You see, I'm still on parole and I can't leave the state."

"How much time do you have left on parole?" asked Pastor Ben.

"About three months."

"What if I could get you permission to go?"

Willie's face showed his surprise. "How could you do that?"

"Well, I've been able to work pretty closely with the justice system, and especially with parole officers. They know we have a good thing here, and believe it or not, most of them want to see men like you succeed. Give me the name of your parole officer, and let me see what I can work out. No guarantees, of course."

A week later, it was all worked out. Willie had permission to be away for two weeks, and with a little arm twisting, Willie's boss agreed to hold his job. Willie was going back to Masonville!

Made
Up
My Mind...

The last time I crossed
that railroad track
I didn't even bother
to look back.
A great big world
just waiting for me;
I was spreading my wings
'cause I was free.
Didn't know returning
could be so scary.
I'm a little excited
but a whole lot leery.
I know I must be
out of my mind,
But I'm going back
just one more time.

W ow! Eight acceptance responses in one week!"
Betty Hartford Hill was both elated and slightly deflated after reading the responses. The one from Millie Davis Cunningham was no real
surprise. She knew all about her. But then there was the one from Sybil
Grayson Welles. Sybil had been her one "friend" in high school, as both
were poor and both were taunted and ridiculed by the other students. Sybil's
attendance almost made her uncomfortable. She represented a part of the
past Betty wanted to forget. She was amazed at Sybil's miniature biography.
The owner of numerous health and beauty salons! Could that possibly be
true? How could she have accomplished that? Then there was Connie Harris
Lark. Connie had come from a coal-mining family with plenty of money,
but no sophistication. She had been good friends with Dorothy Cartwell,
another girl from the coal mines. Connie's response said that she was now a
college professor, a doctor of psychology. Connie's husband was also a professor, Doctor Howard Lark. Bunn Morris, the hunk of the class! Didn't sound
like he had made it too big. She wondered what had happened to the football jock. Then there was Audra James, the preacher's daughter. That's what
they had all called her. She was always mousey, in character and dress. It was
almost like she was afraid someone would speak to her. *Seems like she did have
a boyfriend, though. What was his name?* She had never met Audra's father, but
rumor had it both her parents were real weirdos. Executive secretary in New
York City! Things must have changed for her. *The response didn't say anything
about a husband. Wonder what the situation is there?* Then, of course, there was
Cora Mae Davis. No surprise. Cora Mae, the old maid of Masonville...the
old maid who liked other women's husbands. *Harmon Cline...* Betty looked
at the yearbook. *Oh, yes; he was a star basketball player. I even had a little crush
on him. I had forgotten all about that! Seems like there was some gossip about his
mother.* Says he owns a trucking firm. Definitely blue collar, or less. Betty looked
at the last acceptance note, Mabel Perkins Beck. She had to consult the yearbook again. *Oh my! That girl was loud and crazy. Didn't have a brain in her head.*

Everyone liked her, though. There's just no accounting for taste.

Betty read the responses over and over, trying to envision each one's life. There was just a glimmer of disappointment growing in her. She didn't want anyone to outshine her at the reunion. Oh, well; she was in charge, and she would make sure everyone knew it. *Tomorrow I'll go shopping, because I intend to stand out!*

Millie had fixed a spaghetti supper for Dan, his favorite. She couldn't explain it, but she just had a new vitality. *Does a new hairdo make you feel younger?*

After supper the two went to sit on the front porch, as the weather had been warmer for a few days. Sitting on the porch was something they seldom took the time for anymore. Dan pulled her to the old porch swing where they sat quietly, just enjoying each other's presence and listening to the birds sing. Millie decided to tell him about the invitation.

"Dan," she began. "Do you know how long it's been since my graduation?"

"Umm, let me see... I'm sixty-nine, you're sixty-eight—although you don't look a day over thirty... Why, I guess it's been fifty years! My, how the time has flown."

Millie laughed. "You *are* a smooth talker, Dan Cunningham. No wonder you hoodwinked me into marrying you!"

He frowned. "As I recall, you begged and pleaded with me to marry you, and I finally gave in."

She punched him in the side. "Just keep telling yourself that. They say the memory is the first thing to go."

"Why are you thinking about graduation?" Dan asked.

Millie frowned, dreading to say the words.

"We're having a fifty-year reunion."

"A fifty-year reunion? Wow!"

"I haven't decided about going," Millie added quickly. "What do you think?"

Dan looked at her strangely. "Absolutely, we should go! Would you even consider not going when we live right here?"

"Well, I wasn't so sure about it," she hedged. "Are you sure?"

"I am," he answered, "unless you are ashamed of me."

"Never in a million years would I be ashamed of you, Dan Cunningham. You're the best thing in my life."

"Then it's settled," he said, kissing her cheek as she nestled back in the crook of his arm. "Dan and Millie Cunningham are going to a class reunion. We're going to show those folks what real love is all about."

The next morning Rebekah and Sarah arrived promptly at nine o'clock. Millie had finished the dishes and donned her sweats. She knew she couldn't get out of the exercise.

"Mom!" they called, entering by the kitchen door. "Your darling daughters and personal trainers are here. Are you ready and excited?"

"No and no," she replied, coming into the kitchen.

"Let's show a little enthusiasm," scolded Rebekah. "What could be better than time with your two daughters?"

"Time with my daughters without exercise."

"Did you tell Dad?" asked Sarah, a threatening look on her face.

"I did," Millie replied. "We are going to the reunion; at least we are if I can get time out from the exercises to mail the acceptance."

Rebekah glanced mischievously at Sarah. "Oh, we'll mail it for you on our way home, *after* exercises!"

"Yeah," chimed in Sarah, with a twinkle in her eye, "You may not be able to get to the post office."

Thankfully, the girls had mercy on Millie the first day. They walked three miles and then returned to the house, following up with some stretching exercises.

"I think that will be all for our first day," said Sarah. "I have to work tomorrow, but Rebekah will be here at nine o'clock to walk with you again. She will add some exercises to the routine. Then at two o'clock tomorrow afternoon, you are going for a massage and facial."

"A *what?*" gasped Millie. "I've never had a massage in my life, and the only facial I've had were those I gave myself. I don't want somebody rubbing and pummeling my body."

At this, the girls broke into giggles. "Mom," said Rebekah, "you will love it. It will take about two hours for all of it, giving you plenty of time to go to the hardware for whatever you need to do. You will feel *so good!*"

Millie looked doubtful. "What have I gotten myself into?"

For the next two weeks, the girls exercised with their mother, did stretching exercises afterward, worked out diet menus, and just enjoyed being together. They talked more than they had talked in years. Millie moaned and groaned, but she was actually thrilled with all the attention from and time with her daughters.

One afternoon, with the exercises finished for the day, they sat eating grilled chicken salads. Rebekah looked at her mother for a moment.

"Mom, has Dad mentioned anything about retirement?"

"Retirement?" gasped Millie, laying her fork beside her plate. "Why would you ask that? Is something wrong with your dad that I don't know about?"

Placing her hand on Millie's, Rebekah answered quickly. "No, Mom. As far as I know, he's healthy as a horse, but he *is* sixty-nine. Don't you want time to just relax and do things you've never done before? Maybe travel? Buy a little cottage at the beach, and we could all come down and join you from time to time?"

"I don't think your father would be happy giving up the hardware," said Millie, shaking her head. "What would he do?"

"You two should have had a son to take over the hardware," said Sarah, putting a forkful of lettuce in her mouth. She stopped when she saw the look on her mother's face. Millie had turned deathly pale.

"Mom, what is it? Did I say something to upset you?"

Millie stared down at her salad, still ashen. The girls looked at her and then at each other in questioning silence.

"Mom?" said Rebekah. "What is it?"

Finally, Millie found her voice. She looked at her precious daughters, her eyes pools of tears.

"I know I should have told you girls about this years ago," she said, so quietly they could barely hear her. She took each girl by the hand.

"We did have a son," she said, brokenly.

"You *what?*" they gasped in unison.

"Our first child was a son," Millie continued. "He was born eleven months after we were married…Daniel Adam Cunningham."

Both girls sat in stunned silence.

"He was born July twelfth, nineteen sixty-six," said Millie, as if she was reliving that day in her mind. "He died July fourteenth, nineteen sixty-six."

Tears flowed down her cheeks.

All thoughts of food had vanished. Though they had just heard this news for the first time, the girls' tears almost matched their mother's.

Finally, Rebekah found her voice again. "What happened, Mom?"

Millie stared into nothingness. Her body was present with the girls, but her heart and mind were back in 1966, reliving those horrible days.

"His little heart just wasn't up to the job of living," whispered Millie. "It didn't develop as it should have. We knew before he was born there was a problem, but we thought it was something that could be fixed, as did the doctors. It was so weak that he didn't even cry when he was born. He lived only thirty-four hours. I didn't even get to hold him until after he was dead."

With these words, Millie's tears turned to sobs.

The girls held their mother as they cried together. Finally, as Sarah continued to sit quietly with her mother, Rebekah arose and began putting lunch things away. No one felt like eating.

Sarah patted her mother's hand. "That must have been the worst thing a mother can go through. How did you survive it, Mom?"

Millie smiled. "With God's help and the love of a good man. Your father hurt as much as I did, but he covered his grief to help me get through it. We also did something very healthy; we talked about it. So many couples refuse to talk about such heartache, but we knew that would not be good for us. We needed to talk about our beautiful baby boy, whom we had for such a short time. We still talk about him from time to time. Slowly the healing came, although you never get over something like that. Then too, God in his mercy sent us a little girl just eighteen months later. He sent you, Rebekah. One child never makes up for another—but we had so much love to give, and God sent you to us. Then, two years after that, he sent Sarah to us. We were a family, and we have loved you two every moment of your lives. Then you both blessed us with grandchildren."

"We have always felt your love, Mom," said Rebekah. "I wish we could have met our brother."

Millie wiped at her eyes again. "Perhaps that's part of the reason I didn't want to consider the high school reunion. When you look back at part of your life, you end up looking back at all of it. Some parts are just too difficult to relive. I've never felt like a success. I haven't accomplished anything to make you girls or anyone else proud of me."

"But you have, Mom," said Sarah. "You've always been a strong, supportive mother, always there for us, rooting for us, encouraging us, and you've always been there for Dad. I know there were times when business at the hardware was slow, but you never complained or made Dad feel like a failure. You are a true success."

"And what about your grandchildren, Mom?"

Rebekah did her hands-on-hips routine.

"You are the best grandmother in the world! Who gave Sarah encouragement when Lane was going through so many tests? Who said, 'We will love this little boy, no matter what because he is a gift from God?' Who does Lane love more than anything in this world besides his mother and father? You are a great success!"

Millie could only smile through the tears. To have two daughters like this, she must truly be a success, and most definitely *blessed*.

"Good morning, all!"

Marsha blew through the door of the bar and grill like a predestined hurricane, arms loaded with stuff. The three men stopped to stare, wondering what she was up to this time. They had learned through the years just to step back and wait for whatever was going on in that red head of hers.

"You will notice I am early today," she continued, plopping her paraphernalia down on one of the tables. "Sally is coming in early today, because I have some other things to do."

Bunn placed his cigarette on the ashtray nearby.

"Did it ever occur to you, Marsha, that you are not the proprietor of this fine establishment?"

Marsha didn't bat an eye.

"I know you own the place, Bunny Boy. I'm just the brains and beauty behind it. Now, today ole Marsha is going to begin the campaign to make you into a new person, so you can go to that high school reunion of yours with your head held high."

Bunn picked up the cigarette, took a draw, and blew a ring of smoke.

"First of all, I don't intend to go to any high school reunion. Second of all, I don't need or want a makeover. I'm satisfied with all three hundred pounds of me."

At this, Ray and Gid turned and hurried away to the kitchen, not wanting to be a part of the fall-out they saw coming.

"Three hundred, plus some," said Marsha, hands on hips in her usual manner when she intended to have her way. "That's going to change, however. Today, we start to change all of that."

Bunn didn't even give a reply.

Marsha sat down across from him and opened a spiral notebook. She reached across the table and confiscated his pack of cigarettes, extracting five. She placed them on the table in a side-by-side arrangement.

"You see these?" she asked. "From the time I get here each morning until the time you close up each night, this is how many of these cancer sticks you can smoke. Understand?"

Bunn, glancing toward the kitchen saw Ray and Gid watching the scene. They quickly averted their eyes and began to work. He looked at Marsha.

"And who is going to stop me if I want to smoke more?"

"I am!" she replied with confidence. "You see, I'm doing this for your own good. We are also going to put you on a diet and exercise program. I have daily meals all planned out right here in my handy-dandy notebook. Any minute now, your rented treadmill is going to be arriving; you will use it *religiously*, as well as walk outside each day. Our goal is to lose fifty pounds before the reunion. That's about four months away, so it shouldn't be too difficult."

"You can lose fifty pounds if you want to," said Bunn, taking another draw and blowing the smoke into Marsha's face. "I'm just fine the way I am."

"No, you're not. You are a heart attack waiting to happen, and we are going to whip you into shape...and *you are going to that reunion!* Not only are you going, you are going to look like that Most Athletic, Model Classman, ladies' man you used to be."

Turning toward the kitchen, she shouted, "Boys, Bunn will have two eggs over medium, a slice of tomato, and one piece of toast for breakfast. I brought the sugar-free jelly with me. He can have all the coffee he wants, as long as it's black."

Without a word in reply, the two cooks started the eggs and toast.

Bunn's face began its metamorphosis from unconcern, to disbelief, to rage.

"This is *my* grill, and I'll eat what I want!" he barked.

"Over my dead body!" Marsha shouted just as loudly.

"We can arrange that!" shouted Bunn.

Her reply was to simply plomp a set of scales down in front of him.

"Now get on these scales and let's see what a catastrophe looks like. They're heavy duty, so they can hold you."

Bunn, still red-faced, stepped onto the scales, refusing to look.

"Mm-mm-mm!" she said, shaking her head for added effect. "Three hundred and twenty-seven pounds. We have our work cut out for us. Are those eggs about ready?"

Gid hurried out, plate in one hand and coffee in the other.

Bunn looked at the food angrily and stubbed out his cigarette. Then he glared at Marsha, looked at Gid, uttered an expletive, and began to eat. He didn't see Ray and Gid exchange smiles and head shakes as if to say, "Yep, she's got him."

At ten Bunn turned on the *OPEN* sign. He had many customers who came for a late breakfast and some for an early lunch, so it kept them busy between the two sets. He didn't smoke a cigarette until eleven, just to show Marsha he could wait that long.

Promptly at twelve-thirty, Gid brought him a large grilled chicken salad and set it in front of him.

"Marsha's order?" he asked.

Gid simply nodded, careful to hide the smile he felt coming.

"You eat all of that, and I have some dessert for you," Marsha said as she carried four plates of food to a nearby table.

Bunn snorted. "Probably sugar-free Jello."

Marsha said nothing—but when his plate was empty, she delivered a bowl of cooked apples and cinnamon to him herself.

"See, Bunny Boy? I'm not all bad. Food can be good without having a zillion calories. Now eat up, because your treadmill awaits."

After the crowd died down, Marsha introduced him to his rented treadmill.

"How much is this thing costing me?" he asked, staring disdainfully at the piece of machinery.

"Just a hundred a month. A small price to pay for a healthy attractive new body. Now, we will start out with fifteen minutes. Next week we will go to thirty...three times a day!"

"Oh, I'm so glad *we* are doing this," smirked Bunn. "I have an idea only one of us is going to do the suffering."

"No pain, no gain," replied Marsha. "Or in this case, no pain, no loss."

She walked away laughing loudly. At three o'clock, she yelled for Ray.

"Ray, it's time for you to take a break. Now, on your break, you and Bunn are going for a walk in the fresh air."

Ray looked at her like she had just told him he was dying.

"I don't like to walk," he said.

"Well, learn to like it. You are doing it for a good cause. Now I want you to go south, all the way to Clampett's Warehouse, then turn and come back."

"Clampett's Warehouse!" gasped Ray and Bunn in unison.

"Why, that's got to be three miles!" shouted Bunn.

"No, siree Bob!" replied Marsha, hands on hips again. "It is approximately two miles. We won't get up to three miles until next week. Now, I have some people along the way who are going to be watching for you, so don't even think about cheating; they are going to let me know if you don't pass by. I don't expect you to walk real fast at first, but you are not out for a Sunday stroll, either. Now *go!*"

Like two little boys reluctantly minding their mother, the two men obediently set out for their walk. Both returned about forty-five minutes later, gasping for breath.

"Well, you made it, boys," said Marsha. "Now it didn't kill you, did it? You're going to have to pick up the pace, though. Forty-five minutes! My little eighty-year-old mother could do better than that in her wheelchair."

She handed each of the men a bottle of water, ignoring the murderous look in their eyes. They both drank it, and then Bunn lit up his third cigarette of the day. Only two left.

At six o'clock, Bunn was served a deathly small portion (or so he thought) of baked salmon, green beans, a puny baked potato with sour cream but no butter or salt, and another bottle of water. *Lord, I might as well order my coffin tomorrow.*

Marsha did not let up. This routine continued all week. The one credit Bunn could give her was that she varied his meals and kept them interesting, although most of the time he didn't know what on earth he was eating. The hardest part was the five cigarettes. Then Bunn came up with an idea after he went upstairs each night. Marsha said only five cigarettes...but she didn't say a word about cigars, so each night Bunn smoked a big ole cigar and made it last just as long as he could. He hoped the smell didn't waft its way downstairs.

Exactly one week after the makeover, Marsha came blowing through the door with the set of scales.

"Here we go!" she called. "Get yourself on these scales before you eat breakfast."

Knowing he had no choice, Bunn obediently stopped onto the scales, again refusing to look.

"Well, won't you look at *that!*" she squealed. "Look, Bunn! What do those scales read?"

Bunn slowly looked down. Then he bent a little to look closer, almost toppling from them. He couldn't believe his eyes!

"Well, what do they say?" called Ray.

Bunn looked up. "Three hundred and sixteen pounds! I've lost eleven pounds! Is that possible?"

Marsha smiled as if she had lost eleven pounds herself.

"It certainly *is* possible. Now, see what you can do with just a little effort? Bring him his eggs, boys!"

Marsha kept up the routine, adding more walking as the days passed. By this time Bunn, Ray, and Gid were getting in to the excitement, although Bunn still groaned and complained. After one month and 38 pounds, she announced that he now had a membership in a gym just two blocks away. Bunn didn't argue. At the end of three months, he had lost a whopping fifty pounds. It was coming off more slowly now, but at least it was coming off. The day he weighed in at 270, she set him down and placed the invitation in front of him.

"Now, you are going to take this new body and you are going to that reunion, so you just accept and fill out the other parts. I will put it in the mail."

Bunn stared at the invitation for awhile, as Marsha, Ray, and Gid looked on. Then he picked up the pen and began writing. Marsha mailed it twenty minutes later, before he could change his mind. Bunn was going back to Masonville!

It was Saturday. Most people loved the weekends, but **Audra** dreaded them. She had nothing to do except clean her condo and spend the days alone. It was odd. When she was a teenager, she had dreamed of being on her own, away from her parents and their abuse, and doing whatever she pleased. Now that she was on her own, there was nothing she really wanted to do and the silence was often deafening. She sometimes went to museums but that was boring without someone with whom to discuss the displays. She had some friends at the office, but she never saw them outside work. She was not good with relationships, probably because of her lack of trust in people. Oh, she had dated, especially in her younger years, but it was her self-imposed rule never to date a guy more than once...twice at the most. That way, there was no attachment and no questions to be asked. Robert

Hatcher, the CEO of the company she worked for, had tried to date her for years—before *and* after his marriage—but she never accepted his invitations, although he was a nice guy. His money and position meant nothing to her.

She flipped on her stereo, making sure the CD was not the one with *that* song. As quiet music played, she dusted, picking up the few collectibles she had allowed herself to buy, wiping the cloth across them one by one. As she set the last little Precious Moments piece back on the table, she knocked something to the floor. Looking down, her eyes focused on the invitation.

You are cordially invited...

She knew the words by heart.

Picking it up, she stared into space, her thoughts going back to those days at Masonville High...to her classmates there...to Willie.

"Audra, please go to the soda shop with me after school. We'll just have a shake and then I'll walk you home. Your dad won't find any harm in that."

"You don't know him, Willie. He finds harm in everything. You don't know what he'll do to me."

"Then let me just talk to him. I'll tell him how much I respect you, and how I just want to take you to a movie or for a burger."

"No, Willie. He will never let me go. *Everything* is a sin to him."

Against her wishes, Willie had talked to her father. He showed up at the door one day. She was in her room and her father answered the door. Audra tiptoed to the top of the stairs, just out of sight. He did not speak to Willie, but stood there staring at him.

"Sir, my name is Willie Baker."

Her father made no reply. Willie took a deep breath.

"Sir, I go to school with your daughter Audra. She's a very nice girl, and I would like to take her for a burger this Friday night."

Her father still said nothing.

"Sir, I will treat your daughter like the lady she is, and I'll have her home early."

This time her father stepped threateningly toward Willie.

"My daughter is untouched and unblemished, and I will not have the likes of you touching her or causing her to go astray! Now leave this doorstep, and never show up here again. Stay away from my daughter."

Still standing at the top of the stairs, Audra had heard every word. As he turned from the door, her father looked up. His eyes bored into her, but he said nothing.

Audra's hands shook as she laid the invitation back on the table. Then a smile caressed her face. She would not let her father win. He could not scare her anymore; he had died many years ago, and she hoped he was burning deep in the hottest pits of hell. She would go to the reunion, and she would rid herself of the past and her father's control once and for all. As far as she knew, her mother was still alive; she would lay things to rest with her also.

Before she could change her mind, she picked up the invitation, filled it out, immediately sealed it in the reply envelope, and put a stamp on it. Then she marched triumphantly to the door and placed it in the box outside.

"There, Papa. I won't let you control my life any longer."

As she returned to the living room and to her dusting, she began to hum...

"You've lost that loving feeling, whoa-o that loving feeling. You've lost that loving feeling, now it's gone, gone, gone..."

Audra smiled victoriously as she danced around the room. She almost felt eighteen again.

Harm unlocked the door to Slade and Son Trucking early Monday morning to begin another week of business. He liked to get there at least an hour before any of the other workers, just to get things lined up and get his head on straight. Trucking was a 24/7 business, but Harm had made it a habit several years ago to take his weekends off. He made sure he had trained, reliable workers who could run it during times he was away. He also made it a habit to treat his workers well, and to pay them their worth. He knew what it was like to be treated like dirt, and he would never let himself do that to others.

He sat down at his desk and looked over the weekend papers. Ben Cassen had pulled the weekend shift, and everything was neat and orderly. Like Harm, Ben was a vet and had served in 'Nam. Harm always tried to hire military veterans if he could. Some were reliable, and some weren't. He kept the reliable and let the others go. Every man had to pull his weight; that was just a fact of life.

Leaning back in his chair for a moment, Harm's eyes fell on a picture of Rosalee's father that he kept on his desk. Buck Slade was the only father he had ever known. He taught Harm everything he knew, with a firm hand softened only by the love he felt for Harm. Ten years before the old man died, he had brought Harm in as a partner and changed the name to Slade and Son Trucking. He never truly knew just how much that name meant to Harm. Buck Slade's picture always sat on Harm's desk as a reminder of what he owed this great and generous man.

Harm closed his eyes for a moment...

"Mom, won't you tell me who my father is? I have a right to know. I'm not going to try to see him or anything like that."

"Son, it would do no earthly good for you to know. The man who fathered you has his own family now, and I won't do anything to undermine that. He was no more at fault than I was, and it was my decision to have you and raise you on my own. I have never regretted my decision. You are the best thing that ever happened to me, Harm."

Harm didn't push the matter farther, but he was determined to find out who his father was. One night while his mother was working a five-to-midnight shift at Masonville Cleaners, he went into her room and searched her closet, desk, and under the bed. He knew it wasn't the right thing to do, and that it would break his mother's heart if she found out—but he was a teenager, and desperate to know his heritage. He was just about to give up when he came across some letters in the back of her desk drawer, hidden under some other things. Excited, he pulled them out. His heart told him this was the answer. He opened them one by one and read them, all short letters from a teenage boy confessing his love for his Evangeline. He signed with just his first name, but Harm knew who it was. On one letter he had added his last initial to his name. Harm's stomach did flip-flops. It was obvious the guy knew nothing about her pregnancy.

Well, Harm old boy, you wanted to know, he thought. He didn't know whether to laugh or cry. It certainly wasn't what he expected. His mother had told him the truth. His biological father was a respected man in the community with a family of his own, and Harm knew one of those members quite well. However, no one needed to be hurt from his discovery. The secret would remain a secret.

"Morning, Harm!"

Harm jerked out of his reverie, embarrassed that he had been caught "sleeping" in his office on a Monday morning.

"Have a hard weekend?" Jude Wright was smiling from ear to ear, enjoying Harm's embarrassment.

Harm recovered quickly. "No, as a matter of fact, I had a wonderful weekend. Me and Rosalee took a little trip out into the country, had us a picnic, and got away from the city for a few hours. Guess I was just lost in memories."

It was during their weekend picnic that Rosalee had convinced him that they should go to his high school reunion. He smiled as he remembered her powers of persuasion.

"Fifty years is a long time, Harm. Don't you wonder how much things have changed?"

"Not really."

"Well, I would love to see where you grew up and where you went to school. Don't you want them to know how successful your life has been?"

"Not really."

"Well, don't you want to show me off to all of your old classmates? Aren't you proud of me?"

She had him there. They were going to the reunion.

"Since I met you baby, my whole life has changed..."

As the day wore on, memories from his life in Masonville kept coming back, especially memories of his school days there. Although the adults seemed to look down their noses at him, his classmates never did. Oh, maybe a few, but most just accepted him as one of them. Being a good athlete helped. The girls seemed to be drawn to him, but there was never anyone special. His best friend was probably Willie Baker. He was a little cuss, but oh, man, was he fast on the basketball floor! He could weave in and out faster than anyone Harm had ever seen. He had even seen Willie once after graduation. It was in Saigon, and Willie was just beginning his second tour over there. They had only had about ten minutes to talk, but it sure was good seeing a face from home, especially Willie's. He had looked awfully sad, though. Vietnam could do that to a man. Harm never knew what happened to Willie after that, but he sure hoped he made it back from 'Nam. He might even get to see him at the reunion.

Willie didn't know whether to be happy or sad, but there was no getting around it; he was going back to Masonville and his high school reunion, and he was excited. He had to admit he was scared to death, though. It was just two weeks away, and he shook every time he thought about it.

After Bible study on Wednesday night, he hung back as the others left, hoping he could talk with Pastor Ben. Seeming to sense his need, Pastor Ben headed over toward him.

"Well, Willie, I guess you're getting pretty excited, aren't you?"

Willie fidgeted. "Yeah, maybe. To tell you the truth, I'm scared plumb out of my wits. Maybe I'm just not up to this."

"Nonsense," said the pastor, squeezing Willie's shoulder. "This is going to be a new beginning for you; I have no doubt of that. Have you found a place to stay yet?"

Willie looked blankly at Pastor Ben.

"Uh-oh," said the pastor. "You haven't even thought about a place to stay."

Willie paled. "No, I haven't, but it wouldn't do me any good if I had. I don't have enough money for even a shoddy motel room. I was going to hitchhike there, but I hadn't thought about what I'd do when I got there. Boy, this is a mess."

"No, no!" laughed Pastor Ben. "God always makes a way. He doesn't like messes. Let's sit down a minute."

Willie walked sadly to the nearest table.

"I have an idea, Willie," began Pastor Ben. "We have arrangements here for folks when they are in need. How about if our church pays for your board while you're there, and in turn you can work here to repay the church?"

"But what could I do?"

"How about Saturdays? You free on Saturdays?"

"Yeah, sure."

"Well, we do a soup kitchen on Saturdays for anyone who wants to come by and have a hot meal. You up to ladling soup?"

Willie's face lit up. "Sure. I can do that. But I don't want no handouts, Pastor. Are you sure this is on the up and up?"

"Absolutely!"

"Then I guess I'm all for it," said Willie, with a loud sigh. "You know, Pastor, I guess you're right about the Lord making a way."

"You'll find that the Lord can do a lot of things we never know about until we have the need. Now let me get this all worked out and I'll get back to you. Any place in particular you want to stay while you're back in Masonville?"

Willie thought for a minute. "I really don't want to stay right in Masonville. I don't even know if they have a motel, but maybe I could stay in Baxter. That's a city about an hour away from Masonville. That way I wouldn't run into people before I want to run into them."

"Makes sense to me," said Pastor Ben, nodding. "Just give me a few days, and we'll have you all fixed up."

True to his word, Pastor Ben worked it all out. He made reservations for a week at a decent motel in Baxter. Willie would take a bus from Ohio to Baxter. Then a rental car was paid for during the time he was there.

"Pastor Ben, I can't believe all this. Are you sure I'll be able to pay it back just serving soup?"

"Well, we may have to give you a mop and broom from time to time," laughed the pastor, "but you'll be busy on Saturdays for while. Now, there's another thing you may not have thought about."

"Another thing? What?"

"Clothes."

"Clothes?"

"You'll need some decent clothes to wear while you're there."

Willie sat down in the chair he'd been leaning on. In a voice almost void of sound, he said, "I never thought of that, Pastor. I don't have anything fit to wear during two weeks away, and definitely nothing to wear to a reunion.

I don't even know what people wear to reunions. I'd best just let this idea pass."

"No way. Trust in the Lord, my boy."

"I do," replied Willie, "but I don't reckon God's in the clothes-making business."

"The Lord is in every kind of business, Willie. Remember he made clothes for Adam and Eve. The Lord will provide, my boy. The Lord will provide."

Pastor Ben stood rubbing his chin for a moment, deep in thought. Then, suddenly, he snapped his fingers.

"Thank you, Lord! Willie, let's take a walk."

On the way out the door, he called to one of the men across the room, "Mind the place, Hank! I'll be back shortly. The Lord and I have a mission."

They walked about two blocks and Pastor Ben pushed open the door to a small store. The handmade sign on the door read, *God's Helpers*.

When they left, Willie had his arms full of clothes...*free* clothes.

"I just can't believe this, Pastor," he said.

Slapping him on the back and grinning from ear to ear, Pastor Ben laughed. "Just trust in the Lord, Willie. He'll never let you down. By the way, I have a suitcase I'll be glad to lend you to carry all those clothes."

If he saw the tears on Willie's cheeks, he said nothing.

Sybil Grayson Welles was going back to Masonville. She was going to her high school reunion, and she was *excited* about it. Well, a little scared, too. Her acceptance had been mailed; she and Arthur were making plans, together. Even he seemed excited. It was odd, but their marriage had taken a new turn after she told him about her early life. It was as if Arthur felt needed now, as though he was actually the strong one in the marriage and she wasn't a porcelain doll that he had to tiptoe around.

"Arthur, do you think we could go a few days early and just look over the town and the surrounding area? I don't think there's a hotel or motel in Masonville, and I would like to stay somewhere that's not *too* close...so we can be out and about without running into someone from there. The reunion will be soon enough to renew old acquaintances."

"I was looking at a map earlier," responded Arthur. "There's Baxter, about forty or so miles from there, and then there's Kingston, which would be about two hours from there. What's your preference?"

"Let's stay in Kingston. It's larger, with more places for shopping, and I'm pretty sure there's at least one golf course there. What do you think?"

"Kingston it is, my dear! I'll make all the reservations. You just worry about the packing. You can also write your speech for sharing time. Include plenty about your magnificent, handsome, intelligent husband."

"That will be no problem at all, my love." Smiling, she planted a kiss on his cheek. She had never loved the man more.

I Must Have Been Outta My Mind...

Welcome to Masonville
Population 2,332
Home of the Wildcats

I'm crossing that old
railroad track,
And the memories
come flooding back.
I'm meeting my past
just up ahead,
Recalling a life
I thought was dead.
My Mercedes-Benz
is homeward bound;
Seems out of place
in this one-horse town.
Oh, the memories
are streaming back,
As I'm crossing that old
railroad track.

Bunn hurriedly unlocked the door to his apartment. There had been another letter in his mailbox from Masonville, and he was anxious to read it. Getting a bottle of water from the fridge, he walked to the sofa, sat down, and opened the envelope.

Maybe they've canceled the reunion, he thought, actually surprised to realize the thought disappointed him.

We received your letter of acceptance and your deposit for the meal, and we are excited at the prospect of seeing our former classmates once more. As stated in the first letter, the reunion will be held in the cafeteria of our dear old Masonville High. It will begin promptly at six p.m., but the cafeteria will be open at four-thirty for those who want to come early, look around the school and socialize. After a time of sharing, there will be a delicious meal, followed by music from a live band and dancing for those who so wish. Only three of our high school teachers are still living: Mrs. Rainwood, who is ninety-four and in a nursing home; Mr. Simmons, who is ninety-one, still active, and plans to be with us; and Mrs. Bushmore, who is ninety-four, still active and also plans to be with us. So far, we have heard from thirty-eight of our classmates, of whom twenty-seven plan to attend. There is still time for others. See you in June!

The letter was signed: *Betty Hartford Hill and Cora Mae Davis.*

Mrs. Rainford. Wow, ninety-four years old! She was our history teacher, and a pretty good looker for an older woman. She sure could get into that history stuff. She almost made you like it. And Mr. Simmons, Algebra I and II. Now, that was more my cup of tea. Mrs. Bushmore...Mrs. Bushmore... Now, what did she teach? Oh yeah, English Literature. "To be or not to be...that is the question." Good ole Shakespeare! Definitely wasn't a football player's cup of tea. She was a nice lady, though. Can't imagine her being ninety-four.

Well, I guess it's still on, Bunn's inner messenger board informed him. *For better or worse, it's coming down; and whether I like it or not, I need some more advice from Marsha.*

He was sitting at his table the next morning, coffee in hand, when Marsha arrived in her usual bustling manner, as if thinking OK, *world; I'm here, so we can begin.*

"How is everyone this fine early spring morning? I even heard a bird singing this morning, and that seldom happens here in Chicago. Trains, planes, and automobiles, but not songbirds. It was a smart one, though, telling me how pretty I am!"

She stopped her chatter to look at Bunn.

"Bunny Boy, you look like you are getting ready to go before a priest for confession or something. What's up?"

Bunn smiled. "Nothing's up, Marsh, except this confounded reunion. I'm going to need your help, although I shudder to confess that."

"Just tell Mama Marsha what you need, without the insults," she said, in her usual hands-on-hips stance.

Looking sideways toward the kitchen, Bunn answered in a low voice, "What do you wear to a reunion, Marsh...and don't say a suit! Because I absolutely, positively refuse to wear a suit."

"OK, OK!" she responded. "Don't get your drawers in a twist. Let me think..."

She sat down at the table, the cogs in her brain obviously going 'round and 'round.

"I know!" she shouted, sounding like Archimedes when he ran through the streets shouting, "Eureka!"

"How about one of those swanee shirts?"

Bunn looked at her in complete confusion.

"What on earth is a 'swanee' shirt?"

"Oh, I don't know what they're actually called," she answered. "It's those shirts that are straight around the bottom instead of having a shirt tail hem. You wear it out instead of tucked in. You know, some of them have that Hawaiian look. I call them swanee shirts because *Iswanee,* they sure make a man look good! You could buy a few of those and some khakis. Mix them with some nice shoes, and you'll look like a million dollars."

She paused and looked him up and down pointedly. "Well, a hundred at least."

"How do I get some?" Bunn asked, frowning.

"Just like everything else," she replied, shaking her head in wonder. "At a store! Don't you ever go shopping?"

"Well, I've been needing to, but I hate to buy clothes. Right now, though, everything I own is too large for me."

Hands on hips again, Marsha laughed. "Tell you what, Bunny Boy, you get Sally to come in early this Thursday, and I'll go shopping with you. How's that?"

Bunn agreed and by Friday, he owned a whole new wardrobe of swanee shirts and khakis. Then it was time to tackle the next problem.

"How do you plan to get to this reunion?" inquired Marsha. "Are you gonna fly to the nearest city and then rent a car?"

Bunn leaned back in his chair. "Well, I've been thinking about that. I've decided I want to take a couple of weeks off, rent a car, and drive all the way. I plan to take my time, and maybe see the sights along the way. I haven't been anywhere in a long time. I may even go to Masonville and look around before the reunion."

Marsha looked at him, shaking her head. "You know, dieting and getting more fit has even helped your brain. That is the sanest thing I've heard you say in years. There just might be hope for you yet."

"Who will run the restaurant?" asked Bunn.

"Why, yours truly, of course! I'm the brains around this place anyway. Ray and Gid will be here to help me, and we'll give Sally some extra hours. If we need extra help, we'll get Gid's wife to come in for a few hours each day. We won't even know you're gone."

Out of the corner of his eye, Bunn saw Ray and Gid smiling.

A week later, Bunn set out in a new SUV rental for his adventure, weighing exactly two hundred thirty-three pounds, which looked pretty good on his six-foot-three frame. He had a new haircut and a light tan, but he had absolutely refused Marsha's suggestion of a manicure.

"It just ain't manly."

Stopping several places along the way, he arrived in Baxter three days later, a city just forty miles or so from Masonville. He rented a room for eight days at the Holiday Inn Express. That would give him time to look around a good bit...and he had some looking around to do.

The next morning, he slept until eight and then went downstairs for the continental breakfast. Returning to his room, he showered and donned one of his new outfits. He had a plan. One hour later, he was on the outskirts of his old hometown.

Welcome to Masonville. Population 2,332.

Wow! thought Bunn. *That's being precise. What if someone dies? Do they run out and change the sign?*

Slowing as he entered the town, he looked at each business, each house, each building. *Merrill's Grocery...Sandy's Café...Clip and Curl Hair Salon.* He recognized none of the names, and his heart surprisingly saddened. He drove on. *Darby's Mill and Feed Store.* Now there was a name he remembered. *It couldn't be the same Mr. Darby, though. He would be over a hundred probably by now. Maybe his son took over. What was his name? Sam? Stewart? Stan! That was it! Stan!* Bunn pulled over and got out of the car. A young boy was carrying bags of something to load in a truck.

"Hi there!" called Bunn.

The boy stopped, bag on his shoulders. "Good morning, sir," he responded politely. "Can I help you with something?"

Bunn looked around some more at the place. "I used to live here in Masonville, and just came by to look the town over. Who owns this mill now? Stan Darby?"

"Naw," the boy answered. "Mr. Stan has been retired for several years now. His son Buddy, or Stan Jr., runs the place."

"I guess the years get by before we know it," said Bunn, shaking his head. "Thanks, son."

"The name's Hank," said the young man. "Maybe you remember my grandpa, Henry Pearson. I'm named after him. He used to be the custodian at Masonville High."

Bunn's face lit up. "Why, yes! I remember Henry. He was a good man, son, and always good to the kids. I thought highly of your grandpa. Is he still living?"

Hank's eyes clouded with sadness. "No. Grandpa died just a month ago, at eighty-seven. He was my hero, and I sure do miss him."

Bunn reached over and squeezed the boy's shoulder. "I'm sorry, Hank, but you had a grandpa you can be proud of. It was nice to meet you."

"Nice to meet you, sir." Hank started on toward the truck with the sack of feed, and Bunn headed back to his car. Suddenly he thought of something and turned back.

"Hey, do you by any chance know of a woman named Virginia or Jenny Morris?"

"Why yes," he said, his face lighting into a big a smile. "Everyone in Masonville knows Miss Jenny."

"Knows?" asked Bunn. "Did you say *knows*? Are you saying she's still living?"

Hank plopped the sack of feed on the back of the truck. "Of course. Miss Jenny lives at the Sunshine Rest Home, over on Mason Street. She just celebrated her ninety-fifth birthday last week. The whole town turned out to celebrate."

Bunn patted Hank on the back. "Thanks again, Hank. It's been a real pleasure to meet you."

As he started his SUV, Bunn was grinning from ear to ear. Aunt Jenny was alive! He still had some family!

Slowly he drove on through the town. He stopped a few yards away from Masonville High, parked, and just sat looking and remembering. Most of his time spent there was the best time of his life. He was *somebody*; he accomplished something. Then his mother's face appeared before him. He could see her now, rooting for him as he made his way down the football field, or as he hit a home run, or as he made the winning basket in the Masonville gym. Those were the days! He put the car in gear and moved on, passing another small grocery store and a privately-owned pharmacy, a doctor's office he had never heard of, a lawyer's office, and a hardware store. Then... He could not believe his eyes! There was the soda shop: the one all the kids used to hang out at in the afternoons and evenings. Well, it wasn't the same one, but it was much like it. It looked to be fairly new, actually. *Kitty's Soda Shoppe!* He pulled over into a parallel parking spot and just looked for a moment before he got out. Not allowing himself a chance to back out, he went inside. It was pretty vacant at this time of morning, so Bunn made his way over to the soda bar and sat on one of the 1950's padded stools. A young woman appeared from somewhere in the back.

"Good morning," she said cheerfully, with one of the prettiest smiles Bunn had seen in ages. "What can I get for you?"

"I would like a cherry Coke," announced Bunn, as though he had just made the announcement of the century.

"Coming right up. Is there anything else?"

"No, just a Coke is fine," Bunn replied, looking all around. "How long has this place been here?"

With her back to him as she fixed his drink, she answered, "It was built just two years ago. It's supposed to be a replica of the one that was here years and years ago. My grandma was in high school then, and she remembers it real well."

Ouch! That hurt, thought Bunn. *I'm old enough to be her grandfather. Ouch!*

Swallowing his damaged ego, he asked, "Do you know who rebuilt it?"

"Yes, Bill Hunt. He's lived here forever and ever. He must be sixty years old."

Ouch, again, cried Bunn's ego. *If I don't get out of here soon, I'll be ready for the undertaker.*

The young woman set his Coke before him. "My name's Kendra. Bill Hunt is my grandfather, and his wife, my grandmother, came up with the idea. She graduated from Masonville High way back in nineteen sixty-five, and she said the soda shop was one of her favorite places."

"Nineteen sixty-five, huh? What was your grandmother's name?"

"Ann...Ann Wolfe. Did you ever know her?"

Bunn thought for a moment, then nodded. "Yes, as a matter of fact I did. She was a pretty little blonde cheerleader, and a straight-A student."

"That would be my grandmother," laughed Kendra. "Grandpa says she's still hot stuff."

Bunn laughed as he placed the money for the Coke, plus an extra-generous tip, on the bar and headed toward the door. "It's been a pleasure meeting you, Kendra."

"Wait!" she called after him. "What is your name? I'll tell my grandmother I talked to you."

"Just tell her I'll see her at the reunion!" called Bunn, eyes laughing. This was looking to be an interesting week.

From there Bunn headed back to Baxter and his hotel. The other items on his agenda could wait until tomorrow. He kept thinking about the young girl at the soda shop. *Ann Wolfe's granddaughter... Could I have a granddaughter or grandson that age?* His heart suddenly had a longing, but for what he didn't know.

Leaving the hotel the next morning, Bunn felt invigorated in a way he hadn't felt in years. On the way to his car, he suddenly stopped. *What is that sound?* Then he smiled. The birds were singing! He didn't remember the last time he heard birds sing; then a scene crept into his memory. He and his mother had been sitting on the front porch.

"Why are you smiling, Mother?"

His mother looked at him, a happy, serene glow to her face.

"Don't you hear it, Bunn?"

"Hear what?" he asked. "I don't hear anything."

"It's the birds singing, honey. Can't you hear them?"

Bunn sat unusually still, listening. Then he heard them!

"Yeah, now I hear them!"

"Listen to that one, son. That's a robin! He's talking to his mate."

"Guess I never paid much attention to birds before. You sure seem to like them, Mother. Why?"

She sat quietly for a moment before answering.

"Well, I guess because each kind of bird has its own song, and each kind is different in its own way. Haven't you ever noticed how each is uniquely made? God has made each one special because he cares about them."

Bunn had squinted his eyes in thought. *Why would someone as big and important as God care about a little ole bird?*

His mother reached for her Bible on the table beside her and began turning pages.

"Listen to this, Bunn: 'Behold the birds of the air: they neither sow nor do they reap nor gather into barns; yet your heavenly father feeds them.'"

She turned some more pages and began to read again. "'Are not two sparrows sold for a penny? And one of them shall not fall on the ground without your Father knowing.'"

"Wow! God knows every time a bird dies?"

"Yes, Bunn. And we are even more important to God than the birds."

Bunn stood looking up at the sky lost in those memories, not even bothering to wipe the unhampered tears gliding down his cheeks. He hadn't thought about birds or God in a long, long time. He believed, but he didn't take much time out of his life for God.

Maybe I need to do better at that, he thought to himself.

He started the car and headed back toward Masonville. Slowing again as he entered the town, he once more took in all the sights, in case he had missed some things the day before. On Lewis Street he took a left.

The house where he grew up had changed, but not that much. It had a new blue shingled roof and a new coat of white paint, but the layout was still the same. The front windows still had his mother's flower boxes under them, or at least some like them, with beautiful flowers of all colors growing in abundance.

Mother would have liked that.

Bunn stopped the car on the opposite side of the street, got out, and stood drinking it all in as he leaned against the SUV. He had not noticed the woman bent down working in a flower bed.

"May I help you, sir?" she called, a bit of suspicion in her voice.

She looked to be in her eighties, with her hair pulled back into a bun, and an apron covering the bottom part of her dress. His mother used to wear an apron like that. Suddenly Bunn felt at ease. He walked across the street to the white fence.

"I'm sorry, ma'am," he said, smiling. "I hope I didn't frighten you. I used to live here, and I just came by to see the old place. Haven't been here for fifty years."

A smile wreathed her face.

"Why, you must be one of the Morris boys. Come on in and sit on the porch. I need to take a break from these weeds anyway."

Bunn walked up and took a seat in a blue rocking chair.

"Now you just sit here and relax, and I'll be right back."

She quickly went into the house, coming back just moments later with a glass of lemonade for each of them and a dainty little plate full of cookies.

"My mother used to do this," said Bunn.

The woman took a seat to his right. "Your mother used to do what, son?"

"She used to serve lemonade and cookies to visitors. People don't do things like that in the city."

"Oh, I can't imagine living in the city," she said, shaking her head. "There's too much noise and not enough friendliness. Way too much hoopla. Give me the country life any time."

They sat quietly for a few minutes.

"How long have you lived here?" he asked.

"My husband and I bought the house a few years after your father moved away," she replied, just a whisper of sadness wafting through her eyes. "The house sat idle for too long and was going down fast, as empty houses do. Winston and I wanted to live closer to town where his pharmacy was—we called them drugstores back then—so we sold our little farm and moved here. Now I live here alone. My Winston's been gone nigh on ten years now."

She wiped a tear from her eye.

Bunn surprised himself by reaching over and taking her hand.

"My mother loved this place."

"I believe she died of cancer, if my memory serves me right," said the woman. "Oh, by the way, where are my manners? My name is Sophie Ritter, but you call me Sophie. What is your name, son?"

"My name is Bunn...Bunn Morris," he answered. "I'm the oldest son. It is a real pleasure to meet you, Sophie." He set his empty glass on the small wicker table between them. "I'm sure glad someone bought the house who seems to love it. I can't say there was a lot of love here, but my mother sure loved me and I loved her. My father was a different story."

"Would you like to go inside and see the place, Bunn?" asked Sophie.

"Could I? It wouldn't be too much trouble?"

"Of course not," she replied, waving her hand as though to shew the thought away. "Come along."

He followed her through the door, then stopped, just drinking in the sight. He walked over to the fireplace and stood looking at the mantel.

"My athletic trophies used to be here," he said. "From elementary on through high school, my mother would set them up here. There was a crowd of them."

Suddenly he blushed. "I wasn't saying that in a bragging way. I just loved sports."

Sophie laughed. "There's nothing wrong with a little pride in what we do. You stand here and remember. I'll be right back."

Bunn looked at the comfortable living room. It had changed, and yet it was the same. He could feel the love here. Apparently, Sophie liked books; there were shelves filled with them. He had to laugh as he looked down at the coffee table. There were magazines fanned out on one side...with birds on them.

Sophie returned with a box so large she couldn't carry it. She was tugging it through the hall, scooting toward him a few inches at a time.

"Let me help you, ma'am. What on earth do you have there?"

A smile wreathed her face, and Bunn saw a bit of mischief in her eyes.

"It's something I believe you will be interested in."

Bunn bent down and opened the box.

"Oh, wow! Oh, my!"

Tears poured from his eyes, and he was unashamed. The box was filled with his athletic trophies!

"Ms. Sophie, where did you find these?"

"There's another box in the storage room," she answered, wiping ineffectually at her own tears.

Before he could even stop to think, he threw his arms around her. Then, sanity returning, he quickly released her.

"Oh, I'm sorry. I was just overcome."

"Don't apologize," she laughed, tears flowing down her cheeks. "Hugs are extremely rare for an old lady like me, who never was able to have children. I consider it an honor. Now, to answer your question, Winston and I found these stuffed away in the garage shortly after we moved here. I just could not bring myself to throw them away. It seemed there was just someone somewhere who might need them someday...and here you are."

"I figured my dad had thrown them in the garbage," said Bunn, a hint of anger in his voice.

"I take it you and your father were not close," said Sophie.

"That's putting it lightly," he answered. "That man hated me and everything about me. He never came to my games, or even to my high school graduation. It was almost like he resented me for just being alive. On the other hand, he loved my younger brother. My mother died two months before I graduated, and after graduation I left the next day; I have never spoken to him since. I heard my brother got into some trouble and was in prison, but I don't know what ever happened to my old man. This is my first time back to Masonville in fifty years, and I just came back for my high school reunion."

"I'm so sorry you and your father didn't get along, dear," said Sophie. "Sometimes it's hard to understand why people act the way they do. Maybe coming back will give you some closure, and you can go on with your life."

Bunn visited with Sophie a little while longer, then took his leave with a promise he would come back to see her before he left town. He happily carried his boxes of trophies to the SUV. He couldn't wait to show them to Marsha, Ray, and Gid!

He had one more stop to make. After he left Sophie, he headed toward the southern end of town. There was someone else he wanted to see.

Just moments later, Bunn pulled into a parking space at the Sunshine Rest Home. Before getting out of the car, he sat there looking around for a while. It was a pleasant place on the outside, landscaped with trees and flowering shrubs. He could see different birds flitting in and out of the greenery and enjoying several bird feeders. Taking his time, he got out of the car and ambled toward the entrance of the home. There was no one at the entrance, so he walked on down the hallway. *Guess this is evidence of a small town. In Chicago, there would be all kinds of security.* At the end of the hall, he looked to the right and saw a desk with several people around it. One young woman looked up as he approached.

"May I help you, sir?" she inquired, smiling warmly.

"My name is Bunn Morris," he replied, returning the smile. "Do you have an elderly lady here by the name of Virginia Morris?"

The woman's smile was even brighter. "Why, yes. That's Jenny. Are you a relative?"

Bunn nodded. "Yes, I'm her nephew. I haven't been in Masonville in fifty years, so it's been a good spell since I last saw her. How is she? Is her mind alert? What about her mobility?"

This time the young woman laughed aloud. "Oh, Jenny's mind is sharp as a tack! I hope I'm that alert when I reach her age. She's confined to a wheelchair, although she can maneuver to her bed and back to her chair quite well. Would you like me to take you to see her?"

Before Bunn could even answer, she came around to the front of the desk and motioned for him to follow her. As they walked down the hall, he marveled at the cleanliness of the place and the nice smell. He had never been in a nursing home before, but he had heard some wild stories.

As they approached the open door of a room, the lady knocked lightly. The white-haired woman in a wheelchair looked up from a book she was reading. Looking closer, Bunn realized it was a Bible.

"Miss Jenny, there's a good-looking man here to see you," called the woman. "Just how do you rate a visit from a good-looking guy?"

"Well, honey," replied the older woman, "I guess some of us just have what it takes. Now who do you have there?"

Bunn walked on in. "Don't you know me, Aunt Jenny?"

She squinted her eyes, studying him for a minute, then tears filled her eyes. "Well, 'pon my honor! Is that you, Bunn? Has my boy finally come home?"

He hurried to her and knelt beside her chair. She reached out her arms and he leaned into them. It was the warmest, most content he had felt in years.

"I'll just leave you two to visit," said the young woman, eyes glistening with moisture. "By the way, my name is Carol. If you need anything, just push the button there on the bed."

"Where have you been, my sweet little Bunn?" asked Jenny, voice shaking. "I didn't know if I would ever see you again, or if you were even alive."

"I'm sorry, Aunt Jenny," he responded, wiping his eyes. "I should be horsewhipped. I left here with such anger and sadness I never wanted to see the place again. I have thought of you so many times over the years, but I couldn't bring myself to come back."

"You had so much hate in you, child. Have you rid yourself of that yet?"

Pulling up a chair next to her, Bunn answered, "I think the hate's all gone. It was just difficult to revisit the feelings this place brought. Then I received an invitation to my fifty-year high school reunion. At first, I didn't even consider it, but then my friends who work in my diner insisted I return, and here I am."

He spent the next half hour telling his aunt about his life since his quick departure after graduation. He left out nothing, good or bad, even telling her about the weight loss.

Jenny smiled, more tears zigzagging down her wrinkled cheeks. "It looks like you are finally on the right path. God has a way of setting us back on the path He planned for us. Your father used to come back to see me about once a year, but he died three years ago. They said it was a heart attack. Bunn, he was sorry for the way he treated you...even tried to find you for awhile, but with no luck. The last I heard, your brother was in prison for armed robbery. I was never close to him like I was you."

"Did Pops ever say why he treated me with so much disgust?" asked Bunn. "I used to try with all my might to please him, but it never worked. Then I just stopped trying."

Jenny sat silently for a moment. Then, as if agreeing with her own mind, she looked at Bunn with sadness.

"Bunn, your mother should have told you this years ago, but since she and your father are both gone, I guess it's up to me to do the telling. When they met, Evangeline was already expecting you. Your father fell head over heels in love with her, and assured her he would adopt the baby and treat it like his own. Well, I guess he thought he tried, but he just never could. He gave you his name, but never his heart. Then when Evangeline came down with cancer, he took his hurt and anger out on you. I'm sorry, honey, that you had to suffer so—but if it helps any at all, you were the son I never had. I loved you with all my heart from the first time I laid eyes on you."

He sat beside her, numb from the realization that he was not the son of the man he had lived with eighteen years. Then another thought hit him.

"If he wasn't my real father, who was?"

"I don't know, child," she said, shaking her head. "Your mother never told me, and I don't think my brother ever knew. I know that he died in a car accident without ever knowing about you, so he did not reject you. I also know he wasn't from Masonville."

Bunn visited with his aunt for another hour or so, then took his departure, promising he would come back to see her before returning to Chicago. He had a lot to think about.

He drove back to Baxter and his hotel with thoughts roiling in his head... and yet, there was a strange sense of peace, as well. He couldn't explain it, except now there was a reason for his father's treatment. At least he could make some sense of all those years when his father refused to attend his ballgames, or even his graduation. Bunn took the elevator to the third floor and walked to the door of his room, taking the card from his wallet to open the door. As he started to slip it into the slot, he noticed a man two doors down doing the same. Something about the man seemed familiar. Then he looked up. Bunn stared for a moment, and then reality hit.

"*Harm*? Harmon Cline? Is that you?"

The man stared back at Bunn for a moment, and a wide smile spread across his face.

"Well, as I live and breathe! Bunn Morris!"

The two men met between their rooms, shook hands, and hugged clumsily as only men do. Both were beaming.

It was a beautiful sunny day as **Audra** pulled her rental car into the parking lot of the Best Western Motel in Baxter. She left her car under the check-in canopy and went inside to register. Upon returning, she moved the car to the closest entrance to room 221, unloaded her bags from the car, and headed inside. Audra could have afforded much more lavish lodging, but she was never one to waste money. When you grew up poor, you never forgot the importance of spending money conservatively; at least, she hadn't. She couldn't help looking around to see if she knew anyone, although Baxter was forty miles or more from Masonville. She noticed the Holiday Inn Express adjacent to the Best Western, and wondered if any of her classmates might be staying there. It was unlikely there were any motels or hotels in Masonville, unless it had grown a lot over the years. *Oh, well.* She probably wouldn't recognize anyone after fifty years, anyway. She still had her 1965 yearbook, and planned to look through it before the reunion.

The room was nothing special, but it was clean and would meet her needs for the next week. Audra had plans...if she had the nerve to see them through.

Tomorrow I'm going back to Masonville for my own little reunion, she thought, smiling to herself. *I'll see what the town looks like after fifty years. Maybe I'll even drive by the house. I wonder if anyone lives there... I don't even know if Mama is still alive, not that it matters. I surely don't want to see her.*

She ate at a little restaurant next door to the motel, then turned in early. The flight from New York had been tiring, and she wanted to be rested for the little secret return the next day. Rest was evasive, however; when she did sleep, the nightmares came. The wolves were once more circling her, then they turned into Papa and Mama. Her mother was laughing, but it was not a pleasant laugh; her wolf fangs dripped with blood.

Audra awakened the next morning exhausted. She showered and dressed for the day in a fog. Never one for breakfast, she remembered the little coffee shop across the street and headed there for morning fortification.

"I'll have a caramel latte," she told the clerk.

"Yes, ma'am. That will be three eighty-five."

As Audra reached into her purse for her wallet, it fell to the floor. She bent down to retrieve it, and as she did another hand reached for it.

"I'll get it," said the voice belonging to the hand.

Audra started to stand up, but in doing so bumped the head of her Good Samaritan.

"Ouch! Sorry," said the voice again.

Audra opened her mouth to apologize, but as she looked into the face of her rescuer, something made her stop. Her voice wouldn't come.

"That will be three eighty-five," said the cashier again. "Ma'am, I'm afraid you're holding up the line."

Returning her attention back to the cashier, Audra apologized and handed her the money. Accepting the latte, she turned back to the man who had retrieved the dropped wallet. Something about him was familiar.

"Do I know you?" she asked.

The man stepped out of line so as not to delay other customers, then studied her face for a moment.

"I think you might. Are you Audra James?"

A beam of recognition brightened her eyes. "Yes, I am. And you are Willie Baker!"

"That's me, my lady. Always helping damsels in distress...even when I can't date them."

Despite the memories his remark brought, she couldn't help but laugh.

"I return to Masonville for a reunion after fifty years, and who is the first person I see but Willie Baker!"

Willie joined her laughter. "And I return for the first time in fifty years, and find the love of my life! The gods are surely smiling on me!"

Although trying to appear nonchalant, Audra's cheeks turned crimson.

"Hey," said Willie, trying to give them both time to gather themselves. "How about if I get a coffee and we talk awhile? There are tables outside."

Audra agreed and waited as he ordered. Willie hadn't really changed much since high school. There was no gray in his hair, no stoop in his posture. But his eyes were different somehow: sad, and...tormented.

Willie stared in wonder and shook his head as they settled into seats at one of the tables. "Audra, how have you stayed so young? Life must have certainly been good to you."

At this, the red cheeks from earlier turned white. "Don't allow looks to fool you, Willie."

He waited for her to say more, but no explanation came.

"Where do you live?" he asked.

"I live in New York City. After I left here, I moved to Michigan for a few years, and then on to the Big Apple. I am head secretary to a real estate executive. I love my job, and I'm still working at sixty-eight."

"Married? Family?"

"No. I never married. Therefore, no family: not even a dog or cat. Now, how about you?"

Audra couldn't miss the sudden slump in his shoulders. She looked at his eyes again. Yes, there was that haunted, or maybe tortured, look in them.

"I'm afraid my story is not as productive as yours," he replied.

They sat in silence for a moment.

"Well, let's start with where you went after graduation."

Willie took a deep breath. "I joined the Army."

"Uh-oh! I suspect it wasn't an easy time to be in the Army, was it?" Placing her hand on his arm, she asked, "Were you a part of the war?"

"Yep, two years in 'Nam. Two years of hell."

Patting his arm, Audra took a sip of her latte. *That could explain the eyes.* "Well, it's over and we don't have to talk about it."

Willie didn't reply.

No, Audra, he thought. *It will never be over.*

Sensing Willie's discomfort, Audra changed the subject. "So, did you come back a week early for the same reasons I did?"

"And what would those be?"

Audra looked down at her latte, allowing herself time to respond.

"Well, I guess I came back to see the old hometown and to get some things off my mind: get rid of some baggage, you might say."

"Care to talk about it?"

"I will if you will," she replied, looking deep into his eyes.

"All I can say is, 'I'll try.'"

Audra took a deep breath. "Willie, would you consider driving into Masonville with me as I tell you my life story?"

"I can't think of anything I would rather do, Audra, or anyone I would rather do it with."

The warmth now in his eyes spoke volumes, and Audra felt the most secure she had felt in years.

They tossed their empty cups in the outside trash cans and made their way to her rental car.

"I take it the decision to return to Masonville was not any easier for you than it was for me," said Willie. "Have you been back at all since graduation?"

She shook her head to add emphasis to what she was going to say. "No. I couldn't get away from here fast enough, and never once even thought about coming back...until I got the invitation to the reunion. Fact is, I almost threw it away as soon as I read it. I wanted nothing more to do with Masonville and its ghosts."

"Are your folks still living here?"

"My father died several years ago. I know that only because I searched the obituaries one time in a moment of weakness. I don't know about my mother. I know it's wrong to hate, Willie, but I hated them both with all of my being, and I still do. When I left here, I had to sneak away in the middle of the night with just a few meager clothes and fifty dollars I stole from my mother's hiding place, where I knew she hid money from my father. I knew she wouldn't tell him I had taken the money."

"Was it that bad?"

"Oh, it was much worse... But I'll tell you about that another time. Look, we're entering the big city of Masonville. Wow! Population two thousand, three hundred thirty-two! That's rather precise. Do you think they run out and change the sign every time someone dies or is born?"

Willie laughed. "Could be, I guess."

"Willie, look. There's Masonville High! Look!"

He couldn't help but smile at such exuberance from someone who hadn't wanted to come back to their old town.

"It hasn't really changed much, has it?"

"It looks exactly the same. The school sign wasn't there when we were. You know, I'm actually kind of anxious to see the inside again," she admitted.

"Well, I'll be", declared Willie. "There's the soda shop. Looks like it's been redone, but it's at the same place and looks much the same. Man, how I wanted to take you there!"

Audra's eyes clouded and he was immediately sorry he had made the statement. As they drove slowly on, it was obvious the town had not changed that much in fifty years. It was still mostly a stop in the road. Nearing the end of town, he looked at Audra.

"Would you like to drive by your old home?"

"You mean my old *house*; it was never a home." The anger in her voice was evident.

"Do you want to go by? It might be good for you."

For several moments, Audra was silent. Willie was mentally kicking himself for asking, but he couldn't hold back his next words.

"It might do you good, Audra. I don't know what happened, but it might get rid of some of that baggage you were talking about."

She looked straight ahead. "I don't think anything will get rid of the baggage, but I guess we could give it a try. Actually, I think I knew I would have to do this."

Having made up her mind, she took a right turn at the next intersection and drove slowly past a row of houses. The fifth house set back farther than the others, but she recognized it immediately. It had aged and looked like it had been without care for some time, the white now a dull gray with the paint peeling from the boards. The roof was in terrible shape. With no cars behind her, she stopped in front of it. The memories clamored back with frightening force. From somewhere far off, she heard Willie talking to her.

"Audra, are you OK? *Audra?*"

She jerked back to the present as a car horn honked impatiently behind her.

"Why don't you pull in the driveway?" suggested Willie. "It doesn't look lived in. Maybe we could get out and walk around the yard."

Without a reply, Audra swung the car into the graveled driveway.

"It certainly looks deserted," she said, her voice barely audible.

She opened her door to get out and Willie did the same. She saw the picture window where her mother used to sit and spy on the "sinful" neighbors. The curtains were the same ones that had hung there fifty years ago, now ragged and dirty. The front porch was also as it had been back then, but the paint had worn away and some of the boards looked ready to cave in. It seemed to suit her memories; it was ugly, just like every memory she had of the place. She was never allowed to sit on the front porch alone, because her father would accuse her of "being a temptress."

Willie took her arm. "Let's knock on the door. If no one lives here, we might be able to go inside, or at least look through the windows."

Without waiting for her agreement, he knocked on the door. There was no answer. He knocked again just a little louder. No answer. Just as they were turning away, he saw the doorknob turn. Audra saw it, too, and held her breath.

"What do you want?" asked a frail but harsh voice.

Audra's breath caught in her throat. As frail as the voice was, she recognized it.

Willie, failing to see Audra's reaction, answered, "Excuse me, ma'am. We were just wondering who lives here. It used to be my friend's home."

"Willie," croaked Audra, taking his arm. But before she could warn him, the door opened wider.

"And who might your 'friend' be?" asked the voice. "Well, well, my eyes are failing me, but I think I recognize your friend. After all these years, the prodigal has found her way home. Let me get the fatted calf ready."

Her words dripped with contempt.

Willie looked at Audra, his eyes wide. "Is this...?"

"Yes, it's my mother."

The screen door opened. "Well, since you've decided to grace me with your presence, you might as well come on in."

Audra straightened her shoulders, a look of resolve on her face. "Come on, Willie, let's get rid of some baggage."

Inhaling the mustiness of time, they entered a living room piled with papers and an array of other items that no one had bothered to throw away. It looked like the home of a hoarder, but Audra suspected it was due mostly to sorryness. Other than the accumulation of junk, the room was much the same. Audra could picture her mother and father in that room, yelling at her, telling her what a sinful, wanton creature she was. It was all she could do to keep from putting her hands over her ears to shut out the words that seemed to be emanating from the walls.

Willie, sensing her discomfort, tried to make conversation. "Have you lived here alone since your husband died, Mrs. James?"

Her eyes boring into Audra, Mrs. James answered. "Didn't have no place else to go and no one to help out."

"How long has Mr. James been gone?"

The old woman turned her gaze finally to Willie. "You mean *Reverend* James. My man was a man of God. He was a preacher man."

Audra's face turned red with rage. "He may have been a preacher man, but he was *never* a man of God."

"You watch your mouth, you harlot! You was a Jezebel back then, and you're still a Jezebel now."

"Or so you told me every day of my life!" replied Audra, through gritted teeth.

Willie took her arm again. "Do you want to leave, Audra?"

After a moment of hesitation, Audra looked at him, then walked to the dirty, worn sofa and sat down. "No, Willie, I think I need to work on that baggage."

"How long has he been dead?"

Her mother sat down in front of the picture window in an old rocker. "Let me see...nigh on twenty years now, I guess. I tend to lose track of time."

"And you've lived here alone since his death?"

"'Course I have. Where did you expect I could go? Sure didn't have nobody to help me."

The three sat in silence for several moments, Mrs. James staring out the window. Audra seemed to be coming to grips with her thoughts. Suddenly, she looked at her mother.

"Why did you let my father beat me all those times?"

"'Cause you needed it. You was bad clean through."

"How could you hate a child so much that you gave birth to?"

To the surprise of Audra and Willie, the old woman began to laugh, and her laugh sounded like the cackle of a witch. It seemed to go on and on.

"What is so funny about hating your own child?"

"It's so funny 'cause you wasn't no child of mine! I didn't give birth to something like you!"

Audra turned pale and Willie tightened his grip on her arm.

"Wh-what do you mean?"

"I mean exactly what I said! You ain't no child of mine; I didn't give birth to you."

"Then how did I come to live here?"

"It was the devil's doin'. You was left at our door. I didn't want to keep you—but the reverend, being a man of God, said it was our duty to take you and try to keep you from the gates of hell. He knew you was conceived in sin, and would always be filled with it. And he was right! You was trouble from day one!"

"How do you know I was conceived in sin?" asked Audra, almost a spark of joy in her voice. "Did you know my real mother?"

"Didn't have no idea, though I always thought the reverend knew."

Audra looked at Willie, the joy now obvious in her eyes. "I'm so glad we came here, Willie. I've worried so many years that I might have some of their ways in me, since their blood flowed through my veins. Now I don't have to worry. My blood is not from them. Oh Willie, you don't know what a relief that is!"

Willie put his arm around her, confused but happy with what he now saw in her eyes. Some of the baggage was now gone.

Audra rose from the sofa. "I need to take a walk out back and then we'll get out of your way," she said to her mother.

"Suit yourself. I ain't in no shape to stop you."

Before leaving, Audra walked to a doorway in the house and stood silently, gazing inside, remembering.

"This was my bedroom, Willie. It was as close to hell as anything can get on this earth."

Willie put his arm around her, trying to make sense of her words, realizing something horrible must have happened in this home.

Mrs. James continued to stare out the window as Audra and Willie started toward the door. Then Audra stopped. Something seemed to come over her and Willie saw a newly found peace in her demeanor. She turned and looked at her mother for a moment, seeing an angry, bitter, pitiful old woman. She smiled at the little woman and said, "I forgive you." Then she walked out, knowing she would never see her mother again, nor did she wish to.

When they stepped off the front porch, Audra turned to the opposite side from the driveway. Willie waited as she headed toward the back of the house, seemingly drawn by some force.

"Where are you going?"

Audra did not respond, so he turned to follow her, sensing her need to go in that direction. They walked to the back of the lot, but she kept going down a slight incline. About fifty feet on, she stopped and fell to her knees. Her face was so ashen it worried Willie, but he said nothing, allowing time for whatever was going on in her memory.

"My baby is buried here, you know."

"What?"

"My little newborn baby is buried here."

"Audra, what are you talking about? What baby?"

She bent to the ground as tears spilled from her eyes and meandered down her face. Her hand went to the ground and brushed back and forth as though she was caressing something precious.

"I had a baby, Willie. You didn't know that, did you? No one ever knew, just me and Papa and Mama. He killed it, you know."

Willie's stomach was in knots as his confused mind tried to make sense of what she was saying. He reached out and took the hand that was not brushing the ground.

"Audra, can you tell me about it?"

As the brushing movement continued, her mind went back in time...

"I was only fourteen," she said. Exhausted, she laid her head on Willie's shoulder and the memories came.

"Audra, you need to get cleaned up and wash your hair. Brother Olin is coming to spend the night, and the reverend wants us all to look our best."

"I don't like Brother Olin."

"It don't make no never mind whether you like him or not. You do as your papa says. You best not make him look bad in the eyes of another man of God."

Audra moved to obey her mother, knowing what her father would do if she disobeyed him. She had felt that leather strop too many times before, and the scars were always there to remind her. She didn't like the way Brother Olin looked at her when he came to visit. No one had ever told her about the matters of men and women, but she had heard other girls talk and she had read some things. Brother Olin always found ways to rub up against her, and he would sit and stare at her across the table.

As Audra finished her bath and put on the fresh dress Mama had laid out for her, her mother came into the room.

"I've come to brush your hair, girl."

"I can brush it."

"Your Papa wants it to look extra good tonight."

"Why tonight?"

"Just you never mind. You obey your papa and don't do nothing to make him ashamed."

As her mother brushed her hair, she heard a knock at the front door and heard her father greeting Brother Olin. Chills suddenly overtook her, and her entire body began to shake.

"Why are you shaking, girl? The devil already at work in you? You're a child of Satan, girl, and you always have been. Your papa's gonna fix that, though. Now let's go."

As they entered the living room, Brother Olin rose from the sofa, a gleam in his eyes and a sickening smile on his face.

"Good evening, Mrs. James. Good evening, Audra. My, you have grown up since the last time I was here. You look lovely."

Audra made no reply, and she saw the disgruntled look on her father's face.

"A 'thank you' is in order, Audra."

"Thank you," she responded, barely squeaking the words out.

They soon sat down to supper, and Brother Olin stared at her across the table as they ate. Audra could hardly swallow. After supper, she helped Mama wash the dishes as Papa and Brother Olin talked. As soon as the work was finished, she walked toward Papa.

"May I be excused for bed, Papa?"

"Yes, you may."

Surprised to hear such a pleasant answer, Audra hurried to the bedroom, relieved to get away from Brother Olin's eyes. She had just finished putting her nightgown on and hanging up her clothes when there was a knock at her door.

"Yes?"

"Open the door, Audra."

It was Papa's voice, so she opened the door. Papa stood there and Brother Olin was beside him.

"Audra", said Papa, "for a long time now you have had the devil living in you. As a man of God, I can't allow that to continue. Satan must be exorcised. Brother Olin is going to sleep in your room tonight, and he is going to exorcise the devil from your body so you will be fit to be the daughter of a Godly man. I expect you to do just as he says."

"Papa, please, no! I promise I'll be a good girl. I'll obey everything you tell me to do. I don't want Brother Olin in my bedroom."

"You will do as I say, daughter."

With this, he held the door open for Brother Olin to enter. Then he closed it behind him.

What took place that night was unspeakable horror. Audra screamed, but neither Papa nor Mama came. The next morning, she awoke drenched in sweat, but at least Brother Olin was gone. As the doings of the night flooded her mind, she buried her face in her pillow and cried. When the tears were all shed, though, a change came over her. She got up and dressed, squared her shoulders, and went out to the kitchen. Papa was just finishing his breakfast. She walked to the right side of his chair. Mama stopped washing the dishes and looked at her.

"Don't disturb your papa, Audra. Can't you see he is having his breakfast?"

Audra paid her no mind, but faced her papa, looking straight into his eyes. He did not look at her.

"Don't you ever let that old man in my room again."

Audra spoke slowly, making sure every word was heard.

Papa took a sip of coffee, still refusing to acknowledge her presence.

"Do you hear me, Papa? That dirty, disgusting man will never come into my room again, 'cause if he does, Papa, I will kill him...and then I will kill you. Do you hear me, Papa?"

Her father stopped, his hand in mid-air as he started to take another sip. As he finally looked at her, his face became paler and paler. Something in his eyes told her he knew she meant what she said. He said nothing in reply.

Audra paused in her telling of the story, exhausted from the remembering.

"I'm so sorry, Audra," said Willie. "I had no idea things were so bad for you. None of us at school had any idea. If I had known, I swear, I would have killed the old guy myself. How did you make it through the days at school?"

"School was my refuge," she replied. "I could go to school and pretend to be normal. I could get rid of it all for just a little while."

Willie paused a minute, then realized something else she had said. "Audra, you said something about a baby."

"Yes. That night wasn't the end of my nightmare."

"Did Brother Olin come back again?"

"No, because if he had, I would truly have killed him. I stole a butcher knife from the kitchen and kept it under my pillow. About two months after that night, I began to wake up sick every morning. I didn't know what was wrong, at first. Then my body began to go through changes. Mama and Papa noticed, too, but it was never mentioned. I finally figured out that I was pregnant. At first, I was devastated. Then I began to think about a little baby of my own. I would finally have someone to love, and someone to maybe love me. I began to talk to my baby at night and tell it how much I loved it. I pictured it in my mind a thousand times. As I began to gain weight, I covered it as much as I could. By the time I could hide it no longer, school was out for the summer. Then one night the pains began. When I started screaming, Mama and Papa came to my room."

"Get up and get some shoes on, girl!" shouted Papa.

"I can't, Papa. I hurt so bad. Can't we get a doctor?"

"He yanked me up from the bed, and Mama threw my shoes at me."

"Get these on like your papa said, you harlot!"

"Though my pains were unbearable, I put my shoes on. Then Papa grabbed me and pulled me out the bedroom door, through the living room, and out to the porch."

"You shut up, girl! I better not see any neighbors' lights come on!"

"He led me to this place, half dragging me. The pain was excruciating; I thought I was surely going to die."

Audra rubbed her hand over the ground as tears of remembrance trickled down her face.

"I don't know how long I was in pain, but as they tore at me, Papa kept yelling."

"Be gone, Satan! Be gone from this sinful child!"

"I screamed again and he shouted, 'You are a spawn of the devil, and the devil must be exorcised! Repent, girl! Repent!'"

"With the next pain, my body seemed to rip open...and then I heard a little cry. It was a beautiful cry, my baby's cry. Then there was silence."

"Papa, where is my baby?"

"He didn't reply, but I heard him moving around and I heard a scraping noise."

"Papa, where is my baby? I want to hold it."

"There ain't no baby, girl. It was a thing of the devil, and now it's gone. It will not bring shame on a man of God! You ain't fit to ever have a child, and this should prove it to you."

"I sobbed. My heart seemed to be ripped from my body just as my baby was. I raised my head to see what Papa was doing; he was covering up what looked like a hole."

"Is that my baby, Papa?"

"There ain't no baby! I'm burying Satan. Now shut up, girl!"

"Was it a boy or a girl, Papa?"

"It wasn't nothing! I told you to shut up!"

"With that, he hit me with the back of his hand. It must have knocked me unconscious, because when I woke up again everything was quiet and I was all alone. All I could think of was my baby, and that I would never get to hold it or show my love for it. I had love to give, I just knew I did, but I would never have anything at all to call mine or to love."

Audra sat quietly again, still rubbing her hand over the dirt.

"I never knew what it was, Willie. I never knew if I had a little girl or a little boy. I wanted so badly to have someone to love. I even thought about digging it up, but I didn't have the strength left in me. I knew that it wasn't the right thing to do, too. That little baby was better off dead. It was better off than I was. It didn't belong in this cruel world, but, oh, how I longed to hold it, Willie. Sometimes I still do."

Willie put both arms around Audra and pulled her to him. The rubbing stopped, as did the tears.

"I've never told anyone about this, Willie. It feels good to have someone else know about it."

"It will remain between us, Audra. It's just for us to know. I'm so sorry you had to go through all of that. I wish I could have helped you."

"I *hated* them, Willie. I hated them up until today, when I looked at the woman I had called mother. As I saw the hate and bitterness in her, I realized I didn't want to become like that. I realized, too, that they are not worth hating. Do you understand, Willie, why I'm so glad I'm not their daughter?"

Willie patted her shoulder. "Yes, I do understand. You are nothing like them. You are all that's good and kind and genuine."

He paused, trying to let her absorb his words. "Are you ready to go now, Audra? You look tired."

"Yes, I'm ready."

Willie led her back through the yard and to the car. Though she had been driving, he knew she was in no shape to do that now, so he put her in the passenger side and got behind the wheel. They drove back through the town in silence.

"Willie," she said, breaking the silence. "Could we stop at that little soda shop and get something to drink?"

"Sure, hon, if you feel up to it."

She didn't answer, so he pulled into the little side parking lot. He helped her out of the car and they walked inside hand in hand. The little diner looked like something out of the Fifties.

Willie nudged her toward a table near a window. "Do you want something to eat?"

"No. I think I'd like a cherry Coke."

As the waitress came over to their table, Willie smiled at her. "We'll have two cherry Cokes, please."

They continued to sit in silence until the Cokes came. As Audra took a sip through the striped straw, she smiled. "This brings back some good memories. I wanted with all my heart to come here with you. Better late than never, I guess."

Willie patted her hand. "Is all of that the reason you never married?"

"Yes. I guess so. I just never trusted a man again, and I didn't want another child to replace the one I could never hold. Then, too, I felt so unclean: like I didn't deserve to have love or another child. For some reason, it just didn't seem right. Life has been lonely in some ways, but I guess you can't miss something you never had."

They finished their Cokes and rose to leave. "Willie, there's one more stop I would like to make."

"Fine by me. Where would you like to stop?"

"The funeral home."

Willie did a double-take. "The funeral home! May I ask why?"

"I have some arrangements to make. It won't take long. Will you wait in the car for me?"

Perplexed, Willie sat in the car and waited for Audra to come out of the funeral home. After about thirty minutes, she returned. "OK. I'm ready to go back to the motel. I think we've both been through enough today."

Willie drove back toward Baxter, curious but determined not to pry.

"Aren't you going to ask why I wanted to make arrangements at the funeral home?" asked Audra, a little smile peeping through her eyes.

"Well, I am curious. But it's your business."

"Mama won't live much longer," she said. "I won't come back when she dies, but I paid for her funeral. I made what arrangements I could and the funeral director will make the rest. He will also notify me when she dies. I have no love for her; it just seemed the right thing to do. I guess I actually pity her, Willie, if that makes any sense."

Willie shook his head. "Audra James, you amaze me."

Back at the motel, Willie saw Audra to her room and turned to leave.

"You heard my story today," said Audra. "Tomorrow it's your turn."

Willie smiled and nodded. It had been a tough day, and he could tell she was exhausted. He was a little "wrung out" himself. Willie decided to go to his own room for some rest, though he doubted he could sleep; his mind was going in circles. One thing he knew for sure. He still loved Audra James. Was a life with her beyond possibility? He knew something else now, too: 'Nam wasn't the only hell on earth. *It sure would be nice to have Pastor Ben to talk to.*

Harmon Cline had spent the day showing his Rosalee around the town of Masonville. It was amazing how little things had changed. Rosalee was like a kid at Disney World. That woman could find excitement looking at a manure pile.

"Oh, Harm, is that the school where you graduated? Has it changed much?"

"Actually, no; it looks pretty much the same."

Harm was surprised as he looked at the school. The adjacent football stadium looked newer, but the school was pretty much the same. The old oak and maple trees were a little taller, and there was a school sign out front, but there was little else that had changed.

"Oh, a soda shop! Was it here back then?"

"Yes, but it looks like it's been remodeled."

"Did you go there a lot? I bet you took lots of girls there, and sipped Cokes and flirted. I think I might be a little jealous! Let's go in, Harm!"

They had gone in the soda shop. Rosalee ordered a chocolate sundae with all the trimmings, and he had ordered a root beer float. That's what he remembered ordering back in the Sixties. All the jocks went in there after the games, and the girls flocked in for a free treat and a lot of flirting. Harm had never been serious about any of them, though. Sure, he had dated, but never seriously. The girl he was with now was the one meant for him.

"I do believe this is the first sundae I've ever had in an honest-to-goodness glass dish," she had exclaimed in the soda shop. "It makes them taste better. Don't you think so, Harm?"

It had been a good day. Rosalee was back in the room resting, and Harm had gone out for some bottled water. He was just getting ready to open the door to their room when he saw a man two doors down staring at him.

"Harmon Cline? Is that you?"

Harm looked closer, blankly at first, but then recognition kicked in.

"Bunn Wilson! Masonville's Most Athletic. Well, I declare!"

"When did you get in?" asked Bunn.

"Yesterday. We came a few days early so I could show Rosalee the town where I grew up. Rosalee's my wife."

"Well, I can't wait to meet the woman who snagged old Harm. She must be quite a woman!"

"That she is, my friend. That she is. Say, man, how about if I let her know I'm back, and we could go grab a bite to eat and do some catching up. Rosalee might want to go with us."

"Sounds good. Come knock on my door—room two twenty-three—when you're ready. Bring the missus. I'd love to meet her."

About fifteen minutes later, Harm knocked on the door. He was alone.

"Rosalee said she would meet you tomorrow, but tonight was our time to catch up: talk sports and brag about our old girlfriends."

Bunn laughed. Rosalee sounded like someone he was going to like.

They headed out to a little diner just across the road with outside tables, and over burgers and fries they told their stories.

"I never made it big," admitted Bunn, "and it was my own fault. I left with a lot of anger in me toward my father, and anger and bitterness can just about destroy a person. It just eats away at you until there's nothing left. I didn't even try in college, and then I blamed them when I flunked out. I sunk pretty low, Harm. I'm not proud of it, but it's the truth."

"What turned you around, man?"

"Well, I guess it was a mixture of things. When you sink so low, there's no place to go except up. That is, unless you just want to check out altogether. I woke up in an alley one night, shivering with cold and so hungry my gut felt on fire. I could even smell an awful odor that I realized was me, and I knew at that moment something had to change. Luckily, or maybe it was God's all-seeing power, I met a man named Pastor Bob. Then I met another man who befriended me later on, and he became like the father I never had. Actually, though, I guess it was God who turned me around. What about you, Harm? You seem really happy. What did you do after school?"

"I joined the Army."

"The Army! Wow! That must have been a tough time to be in the Army!"

"It was tough, but I guess it made a man of me. I let go of things back here because I didn't have time to think about them. I was too busy trying to stay alive. 'Nam left its scars, though. If it hadn't been for Rosalee, I don't know what might have become of me. We both got involved in church, and that helped immensely."

"Were you scared? Or is that a dumb question?"

"No, it's not dumb, and yes, I was scared to death most of the time. It was hot as blazes, with unbelievable humidity and the biggest insects you could ever imagine meeting up with. Red ants were the worst, man! We called them 'red devils.' When they got on you, they would just about eat you up. Then there was that awful orange mist that we now know as Agent Orange. I guess we were being killed by both sides."

"What about the people you were fighting? Were they as inhuman as I've heard?"

"Probably even worse. They could be a few feet away from you in the jungle, and you would have no idea they were there until they were all over you. And even worse, it was hard to tell the good guys from the bad guys until it was too late. They all looked alike to dummies like me. It was a real relief to leave that place. The sad part is, many came back in coffins. Some of them were good friends."

Bunn felt that it was time to change the subject.

"How did you meet Rosalee?"

Harm proceeded to tell him the story of meeting Rosalee, marrying her, and becoming the owner of a trucking company.

"Great day! You are one lucky dude, Harm!"

"I like to call it blessed, because God has richly blessed me. You know, I didn't want to come to this reunion, but Rosalee talked me into it. Now I'm glad I came. It's really good to see you again, man. Life doesn't always turn out the way we plan, but sometimes God has something better in store. He had Rosalee for me, and I will always be grateful for that. Say, have you heard anything of Willie Baker since high school?"

"No, sure haven't. Man, he was fast on the court, wasn't he?"

"Yeah, he sure was. I saw him once in Saigon, but we only had about ten minutes to talk. Maybe he'll show up at the reunion. Sure would like to talk to him."

They talked on for another half hour and decided it was time to turn in.

"I want you to meet Rosalee, Bunn," said Harm as they parted. "How about if we have breakfast together in the morning, about nine? There's a nice little breakfast place just down the street."

"I'll be looking forward to it," replied Bunn, "and I'm looking forward to meeting the woman who has made your life a happy one."

Willie had gone to sleep thinking about Audra, and he woke up with her on his mind. That sweet girl had been through hell. She had to be strong, to live with those nightmares and still make a success of her life. Why hadn't he done better with his?

I wonder if things would have been different if Audra and I had gotten together. What if we had married? What if I had never gone to 'Nam? What if I had never gotten mixed up in drugs? What if I had never gone to prison?

Willie shook his head. If he had a dollar for every *what if* and *maybe* in his life, he would be one rich man.

What if I asked Audra to marry me now? Would she say yes?"

"You old fool!" he said out loud.

I don't have anything to offer her. She's white collar, and I've never even made it to blue collar. I barely make enough to exist. I can't ask Audra to live in a rat-infested pig sty and eat bologna and molded bread! Geez Willie, you're still on parole! Then there are the nightmares...

There was no hope. Willie had to accept that.

He showered and got dressed. He was meeting Audra for coffee, and possibly to confide in her. Yes, he owed it to her to tell her everything.

Even 'Nam? I don't know if I can do that.

She was sitting at an outside table waiting when he arrived, coffee and bagels ready.

She smiled. "Morning, sleepyhead."

Lord, he loved that smile. "And good morning to you. Did you rest well?"

"As a matter of fact, I did. Best night of sleep I've had in a long, long time. Facing your ghosts can be quite therapeutic. Thanks for going with me, Willie."

Unable to restrain himself, Willie reached over and took her hand. "My pleasure, ma'am. My pleasure."

They sipped coffee and ate their bagels in silence for a moment. It was the silence of contentment.

Audra suddenly broke the silence. "All right, Willie boy; I believe you have a story to tell me, so let's hear it."

Willie's heart quickened and he took a deep breath. "It's not a pretty story, Audra."

"Neither was mine. I'm listening. Where did you go after high school?"

"Well, after leaving Masonville only a week following graduation, I went to Florida and worked here and there for a while. I loved the weather but saw no real future there, so I joined the Army."

Audra squeezed his hand. "Were you in the war?"

"Yep. Afraid so."

Willie was about to continue when he suddenly stopped. Then he stood up, staring just down the sidewalk at three people about to enter the café. It was about this time that one of them looked his way.

"Willie? Willie Baker? Is that you?"

"Harm?"

They walked toward each other as the third man followed. Then Willie recognized him, too.

"Bunn Wilson?"

"It surely is, Willie."

Both men grabbed Willie and drew him into a three-man bear hug, unable to hide the tears. The two women looked on in amusement. Others on the street stopped to stare, then smiled and walked on, realizing old friends were reuniting.

"We were just talking about you last night, Willie, hoping you might come to the reunion. Me and Bunn just ran into each other yesterday. We're actually staying at the same hotel."

Harm motioned for Rosalee, and she joined them.

"Willie, this is my wife, Rosalee. Rosalee, this Willie Baker, fastest guy ever on the basketball court."

Rosalee smiled. "It's nice to meet you, Willie. Harm has talked a lot about you."

At this time, they all looked over at the table where Willie had been sitting.

"Aren't you going to introduce us to your lady?" asked Bunn.

"I think you both already know her," replied Willie, a sly grin on his face.

They both looked more closely.

"It can't be..." Harm marveled. "*Audra James? Is that you?*"

Bunn stood with his mouth open.

Audra arose, smiling. "You are right, Harm. I'm Audra James, known in high school as the 'preacher's daughter.'"

"Wow!" declared Bunn. "You sure look younger than the rest of us."

Remembering his manners, he added, "Except Rosalee, of course."

"Too late, buddy," laughed Rosalee. "You've already dug your hole."

The others laughed as Bunn turned red.

Harm looked more closely at Willie and Audra.

"Are you two..."

Willie and Audra looked at each other perplexed.

"I think he's trying to ask if you two are married," laughed Rosalee.

"Married? Oh, no! We just ran into each other yesterday. Hadn't seen each other in fifty years."

"Why don't you get your food and join us?" suggested Willie. "We'll pull some chairs over."

They were soon all gathered around the outside table, each telling a portion of their story since graduation. Honesty prevailed because, after fifty years, they had nothing to hide anymore. Yet Willie had remained noticeably quiet.

"You know, I'm reminded of that Statler Brothers song," said Bunn. "'Things get complicated when you get past eighteen.' I guess it did for all of us, but we all had our dreams."

"Dreams are sometimes just that," injected Audra. "Life is more than just dreams. There are some hard knocks along the road."

"Willie," said Harm, "you've been awfully quiet. Is something wrong?"

Willie looked at Audra and she nodded, seeming to read the question in his eyes.

"I was just about to tell Audra about my life when I saw all of you. I guess I can just tell it to all of you and get it over with. It's not a pretty story, but I guess I need some closure."

Audra reached over and covered his hand with hers. Harm placed his hand on Willie's shoulder.

"We're here for you, bud. No judgment will come from us."

"As I was telling Audra, after I left here, I went to Florida for a while. But there was really nothing there for me, so I joined the Army. I remember seeing you in Saigon for just a few minutes, Harm. Man, did I want to talk to you! It was exciting just to see a familiar face, but I had a helicopter to catch. Had to head back out into the 'heavenly' jungles of 'Nam."

He paused for a moment as though gathering more strength. Audra squeezed his hand and he continued.

"Vietnam was pretty rough. I guess you know that, Harm."

Harm nodded and his eyes took on a sad, faraway, knowing look.

"I did two tours over there," said Willie. "I know I must have been insane, but I just didn't know what else to do. I was a tunnel rat."

Harm gasped. "Lord, Willie! Man, you had the roughest job over there! I've heard the stories. Just the thought of it always gave me the creeps. It was bad enough in the jungle, but..."

"I'm sorry to interrupt," said Rosalee, "but what is a tunnel rat?"

"Almost what it sounds like," replied Willie. "The 'Congs had a labyrinth of tunnels all over the place. Those sneaky little demons could crawl through those tunnels faster than a slithering snake. They moved equipment and information through them as well as themselves. The tunnels were barely wide enough to crawl through, but they would sneak through them and just suddenly show up where we were and come down on us. As tunnel rats, we had to crawl through them to gather what information we could—and close off the tunnels when we could. Like I said, the tunnels were barely wide enough to crawl through, and there was no way to turn around. You crawled forward going in and you crawled backward to get out. That job was only for little guys."

"Lord, I can't imagine," said Bunn, his face white. "I'm claustrophobic. I would have smothered to death in there. I smother now just thinking about it, but of course, with my size I couldn't have fit in one. Don't know how you did it, Will."

"I guess we sort of got used to that part of it," answered Willie, "but there were other parts we never got used to. You just never knew what you were going to find in those tunnels. You see, they knew we were locating some of the tunnels, and they wanted to make sure we didn't come out alive. I think it even pleased them that we found them, so they could wreak more of their evil. With so little space, we couldn't carry anything but a gun and a flashlight, sometimes a knife. They would put pit vipers in there, and we would be upon them before we knew it. We called them 'three-step' snakes. Once they bit you, three steps and you were dead. In our case, three feet of crawling backward and you were dead. I almost got it a few times."

"What did you do?" asked Rosalee.

"I shot them. The only problem to that was the loudness of your gun in a tunnel like that could just about destroy your eardrums."

They sat in silence a minute, giving Willie time.

"The worst part was when they put punji sticks in there. You might crawl over a buried string or something else that would trigger the sticks. They had... poison on them and they stabbed right into you."

Harm nodded. "Yeah, I had some experience with them. They would put them in a hole in the ground, and cover it over with branches and leaves. Sometimes two or three men would fall in at one time. I can still hear the screams. They never came out alive. Those sorry 'Congs had demon brains, and they weren't afraid of anything. Life didn't seem to have any meaning to them."

"The worst time I ever had," continued Willie, "was when they put a baby in a tunnel."

"A *baby?*" Rosalee gasped. "Why would they put a baby in there? That's just pure evil. That's not even human!"

"It was big enough to crawl. They would tie a string around the baby's ankle and it would crawl so far through the tunnel. When we met up with it, we could either kill it or back out. Once I had my gun out and ready to shoot before I realized what it was. I backed out of there fast. And, no Rosalee, they were not human. They enjoyed seeing us suffer and be blown apart, and die. We were fighting a people with no heart."

Everyone shook their head in silence, trying to even imagine such atrocity.

"Anyway," continued Willie, "when I left 'Nam, I wasn't the same little Willie Baker I had been before. The nightmares were horrendous, and people back here in the states treated us like dirt. I guess the war was all wrong, but we were just serving our country. I had a hard time holding down a job because after a night of refighting the war, I was too strung out to get out of bed. No boss wants to keep a man who doesn't show up for work. To deal with it all I got into drugs. I just wanted to make the nightmares go away. I slept in the streets and dug into garbage cans for food. I sank pretty low, but it got lower. I went for counseling a few times. It helped for a month or two, and then I'd go back to the drugs. The government didn't do much to help us back then. You didn't even hear about PTSD. We were pretty much on our own. I was put in jail a few times, but only for a night or two. Then, about two years ago, I was caught with drugs on me. I spent eighteen months in prison, and I'm still on parole. I had a pastor friend who talked the parole board into allowing me to come for the reunion. The pastor thought it might help give me closure. By the way, Pastor Ben also introduced me to Jesus, and I was saved. Been going to church and trying to serve the Lord ever since. So, my friends, that's the story of Willie Baker, Most Likely to Succeed. I had no plans to come back to Masonville, and definitely not to a class reunion. I had no money to get here, and not even clothes to wear, but I'm beginning to think it's the best move I've made in years."

He looked at Audra as he spoke the last words.

Again they were silent, each pondering the last fifty years.

"So maybe," said Harm, "God had a hand in us coming back for this reunion. None of us wanted to come, yet here we are. I don't know about you guys, but it's been good for me, and we haven't even had the reunion. Just seeing all of you has made it a good decision."

"I don't think the actual reunion is the important part," said Bunn. "I think this right here is the important part, and what Audra faced yesterday, and what I faced in going back to see my old home and talking with Aunt Jenny. I think that's what God had planned for us. 'God moves in mysterious ways, His wonders to perform.' That's what my mother used to read to me from the Bible."

"We all had things we needed to let go of," said Audra. "Yes, we made the right decision."

Arthur and **Sybil** arrived in Kingston three days before the reunion. They rested the first morning, then set out to explore the small city, walking hand in hand as they visited clothing stores and craft shops. The second day, they went to Masonville. Sybil showed Arthur around the small town; they even drove by the little house where she had once lived. It was rundown and empty, looking even sadder than she remembered it. At one time, she would have been too ashamed for Arthur to see it; now, there was a relief in it. As they sat in the car, Arthur held her hand in silence, allowing her to go back in her memories. He could not imagine the Sybil he knew living in a house like that, or even a town like this. They returned to Kingston for dinner, and as they dined Arthur asked what her plans were for the last day before the reunion.

Sybil didn't answer for a few moments.

"Syb, don't you know what you want to do tomorrow?"

"Yes," she replied, but the color had drained from her face.

"There's someone I need to go see, Arthur, someone I should have gone to see many years ago. But there's a story I must tell you."

"I'm listening, Syb. Who do you want to see?"

"I need to go see Charlie."

"Charlie? Who's Charlie."

"He's my son."

This time Arthur turned pale. "Your *son?* You've never told me anything about a son, Syb."

"I've never told anyone. Even my parents never knew. Even his father never knew."

"Again, I'm listening."

There was no condemnation in Arthur's voice. There was only concern.

"After graduation, all I could think about was getting away. I worked on in Masonville for a few months at a clothing store, just to get enough money to leave. I had to keep my money hidden from my father so he wouldn't gamble it away. Then I went to Hartsburg and got a job in a factory there. It didn't pay much, but I had enough for food and rent. I didn't even have a car, but I lived close enough to walk. Then I met Joe. He 'wined and dined me,' as the saying goes, and he made me feel important. He made me feel *loved.* I had never felt either before, and I longed to be loved. I longed to be somebody. We married two months after we met and bought a tiny little house. We were happy...for a little while. Then Joe got restless. He wanted to have fun, but we didn't have any money for fun. I began to see my father in him. Soon I got pregnant, and Joe said, 'That wasn't part of the plan.' Then Joe left; a month later, I got divorce papers. I signed them and never heard from him again. I worked on until it was time for the baby, then a woman I worked with told me of a home for women who needed help. It was for women who did not plan to keep their baby, however. I felt I had no choice. There was no way I could take care of a child. I couldn't even take care of myself. There was no way I wanted my child to have to live a life like I had lived. Charlie was born August fourth, nineteen sixty-six. He was a Down's Syndrome baby."

"Oh, my love," whispered Arthur, pulling Sybil close. She was quiet for a moment.

"The first few days were touch and go. He came so close to dying; God forgive me, Arthur, but there was a part of me that hoped he would. I couldn't see what kind of life he could have. But my Charlie lived. He was a fighter. The social workers came and took him away, but no one would adopt him, I guess, so they finally put him in a home for mentally challenged children. We didn't know a lot about Down's Syndrome in those days. We didn't realize what a positive part of society they can be. I went to the home about six months after he was born and they let me see him. He was so beautiful, and I never felt more at peace than when I held him. Mrs. Long, the head lady at the home, told me I could keep in touch and could see him when I wished, but I never went to see him again. I knew it would hurt too much...yet not seeing him hurt, too. I have sent money every month since that visit, though, and for a long time she sent me a picture of him once a year. He is forty-nine now, quite a long age for one with Down's Syndrome. That's really why I wanted to come back, Arthur. Well, the main reason. I need to see Charlie."

"Then tomorrow we will go see Charlie," said Arthur as he put her hand to his lips.

They ate breakfast at nine the next morning and headed to Evanston, about ten miles from Kingston, to Happy Hearts Village. Mrs. Long had died several years earlier, and Sybil had only spoken to Mrs. Marshall by phone. The receptionist immediately showed Arthur and Sybil to her office.

Mrs. Marshall arose with a smile and shook their hands. "It is a pleasure to finally meet you, Mrs. Welles. Charlie is such a dear man, and quite a help to us. I do thank you for all your contributions; they have helped immensely. Charlie loves gardening, and I always use part of your donations for that endeavor. As a matter of fact, he's working outside now. Would you like to go see him?"

Sybil stood quickly. "Oh, yes! Let's go now."

As they exited through a side door, they saw a young man was clipping some dead blooms from a beautiful plant. They stopped to watch him for a minute. He was humming as he worked.

"Charlie always hums to his plants," said Mrs. Marshall, smiling.

They walked on out to where Charlie was working.

"Charlie," called Mrs. Marshall.

He turned around with a bright smile on his face.

"Charlie, I have some visitors who want to see your beautiful garden. This is Mr. and Mrs. Welles."

"It's nice to meet you," Charlie said, his smile even brighter. "Do you like plants?"

Sybil returned his smile. "I love them, Charlie, but I'm not as good with them as you are. Yours are so healthy."

"You have to hum to them," said Charlie. "They like humming."

He walked around the garden showing them different plants, knowing the name of each.

"These are petunias, and these are begonias, and these are geraniums..."

"What is your favorite of all the flowers, Charlie?" asked Arthur.

"I like mewygolds," answered Charlie, having trouble with the pronunciation. "They are bright and happy, and they last a long, long time. Bugs don't like them, and that's a good thing."

As they all laughed, Sybil carefully reached over and put her hand on his shoulder.

"Charlie you have a wonderful garden. You must be very happy here."

"I like my plants," he replied with a smile, "and I like Mrs. Marshall, and Mr. Phillips, and Mr. Lawrence, and Tommy, and Carl, and Alice... Did I leave anybody out?" he asked, looking at Mrs. Marshall.

She laughed. "No, Charlie, I don't think you left anyone out."

"Charlie, how would you like to go out to eat tonight with Arthur and me? We'd like to hear more about your flowers and your life here."

Charlie looked at Mrs. Marshall, a question in his eyes.

"It's OK with me, Charlie, if you would like to go. You know, Mrs. Welles sends us money every month and part of that money goes for the greenhouse. I think she deserves to hear about it."

"OK, I would like to go," said Charlie. "Can we go to McDonald's?"

Arthur and Sybil looked at each other, taken completely by surprise. Sybil had never eaten at a McDonald's in her life.

Arthur regained composure first. "We can absolutely go to McDonald's, Charlie. We'll pick you up at six."

Arthur and Sybil took their leave, promising to return promptly at six to head to McDonald's. It was easy to see Charlie was happy, and they left with lighter hearts.

At six, Charlie was waiting for them, so they headed out. They kept up a steady conversation.

"Tommy has a mudder and a fadder," said Charlie, suddenly. "They come and get him and he goes home with them every weekend."

Sybil's heart gave a lurch. "Do you wish you had a mother and father, Charlie?"

"Naw! Then I'd have to leave my flowers and they wouldn't have anybody to hum to them."

Arthur and Sybil laughed aloud. They drove quietly for a few moments.

"Knock, knock," came from the backseat.

Sybil was speechless, but Arthur was quick to reply.

"Who's there?"

"McDonald's."

"McDonald's who?"

"McDonald's is old. How about you?"

They all laughed and tears sprang into Sybil's eyes.

Charlie decided to try it again.

"Knock, knock."

This time Sybil replied, "Who's there?"

"Dwayne."

"Dwayne who?"

"Dwayne the bathtub, I'm dwowning!"

This continued all the way to McDonald's, and Arthur and Sybil laughed so much their sides were hurting.

In McDonald's, Charlie stepped right to the counter and ordered.

"I want two Big Macs, a large order of fwies, and a large Coke."

"What do you want, Syb?" asked Arthur.

"I don't know. What do people order at McDonald's?"

"Shall I order for you?"

"Yes, please."

Sybil found a booth and soon Arthur and Charlie brought the food and drinks.

Arthur began opening his burger.

"We forgot to say the bwessing," Charlie said, his burger still wrapped.

"Oh, sorry," replied Arthur. "Charlie, would you say our blessing?"

"Lord, we thank you for this food and for my flowers, and for McDonald's. Amen."

The blessing said, they all opened their burgers. Sybil looked at hers hesitantly, then lifted the top bun. She removed the pickles, and Arthur laughed quietly as the ketchup covered her perfectly manicured nails. She saw him laughing and gave him one of her threatening looks. Finally, she bit into the burger. Arthur watched her chew slowly. Then her eyes lit up.

"Charlie, I think I like Big Macs!"

Charlie shook his head. "That's not a Big Mac. That's a Quarter Pounder!"

It was Arthur's turn to laugh.

"Knock, knock," said Charlie, between bites.

"Who's there?"

"Eyesore."

"Eyesore who?"

"Eyesore do love you!"

Through tears, Sybil replied, "And we sure do love you, Charlie."

After they finished their burgers, Charlie and Arthur had a chocolate ice cream sundae. After numerous more knock-knock jokes, they returned Charlie to Happy Hearts and headed to their hotel.

"What a great evening!" declared Sybil.

"Best ever," replied Arthur. "That boy is a doozy!"

"Did I make the right decision those many years ago, Arthur?"

He squeezed her hand. "Yes, my love. I think you made the right decision. Charlie is definitely happy."

"Knock, knock," said Sybil.

Arthur looked at her in amusement. "Who's there?"

"Ula."

"Ula who?"

"Ula-ight up my life..."Sybil sang the last part.

"And you light up mine," said Arthur, and his eyes showed that he meant it.

"I'm glad we came back for the reunion," said Sybil. "I faced my ghosts, and now I can face life with reassurance."

They drove on in silence for about thirty minutes, until Sybil spoke again.

"It's all fake, Arthur."

"What's fake, Babe?"

"Our life. It's all fake."

"Do you mean you and I are fake?"

"Not our feelings or our love, that's real. But the life we lead is all fake, and I don't want it anymore. We're supposed to go to France in two weeks, and I don't even want to go. We go to Italy, Greece, Spain, Hawaii, and it means nothing. It just makes us look wealthy. Well, wealth doesn't make you happy."

"What makes you happy, Sybil?"

"You...and Charlie."

"What would you like to do, Sybil? I want both of us to be happy?"

"I want to sell it all and be where we can see Charlie more often. We don't have a lot of time left, Arthur, and I just want to be with the two people I love most in the world."

"I want that, too," said Arthur, squeezing her hand. "I say we sell the salons and move to Evanston. That way we can be near Charlie, and we can lead a life that's not fake."

"Do you mean that, Arthur."

"Absolutely."

Fifty Years
and
Crazy!!!

They say when you leave
you can never go back.
You can't re-cross
that railroad track.
For just one night
we faced the past,
Shared memories that
will have to last.
From an innocent time
to a world of strife,
Some faced regrets;
some found new life.
We're leaving again,
not looking back.
We're crossing that
old railroad track.

Millie could hardly believe her eyes as she and Dan entered the old high school cafeteria, to be greeted by Betty Hill in all her self-appointed glory. Actually, Betty looked quite nice and was unusually friendly. The cafeteria was beautifully decorated; Betty had spared no expense; this was no quick balloon and crepe paper job. There were flowers everywhere, and there were even cloth napkins. *Wow!* Millie thought. The room, minus the decorations, hadn't changed that much, but the people... Who were these strangers? There were people there with white hair, red hair, blonde hair, no hair, and even purple hair. Gone were the youthful, high school figures of the people she had known. These were *old* people. No one was flitting across the room as they once had, instead maneuvering carefully and slowly with limps, bent backs, canes, and walkers. She looked at Dan, who seemed to be equally amazed.

"Are we this old?" he asked. "Do we have the wrong reunion?"

Just as she was about to agree with him, the hopeful idea was put to rest by someone calling her name.

"Yoo-hoo! Millie Davis! Is that you?"

A short round lady with bleached hair was descending upon her.

Lord, help me to know this woman, Millie prayed.

"Millie Davis, you are a sight for sore eyes!" the woman squealed. As she came closer, her name tag was visible. *Linda Marshall Conway! Thank you, Lord!*

"Bet you didn't recognize me," Linda teased, smiling.

"Well, not at first," confessed Millie. "How are you, Linda? You are looking well."

"Oh, I pay a lot to look this way," laughed Linda. "Botox and the scalpel have become my friends."

You're paying too much, thought Millie, then quietly scolded herself.

"I hear you still make your home here in our little hometown," said Linda.

Millie couldn't help but detect a little bit of condescension.

"Yes, Dan and I have lived here all our lives. It's where our family is, and where we feel at home. What about you, Linda?"

"Oh, Walter and I live out near D.C.," she replied. "I don't think I could live in a small town again. Walter works at the Pentagon, and I own a travel agency. We stay busy, busy, busy!"

"Do you have children?" asked Millie.

"Oh, no," she answered, swishing her finger from side to side to emphasize her answer. "We have no time for children. We love our work, and we love to travel. In fact, we've seen most of the world. We don't even have a dog."

Millie suddenly felt sad for Linda. She couldn't imagine a life without children.

"Oh, excuse me," said Linda, hurrying away. "I believe I see someone else I know."

Dan looked at Millie to see her reaction to her old classmate. She simply rolled her eyes, shook her head, and smiled.

"I believe I saw your friend Mary and her husband come in while you were talking," he said, nodding toward the other side of the room. "Want to go sit with them?"

"Yes, let's do. I told her I would watch for her."

As planned, Bunn, Harm, Rosalee, Willie, and Audra found their table together. Well, it wasn't really *their* table, as name cards had been placed on all the tables; Bunn and Harm simply changed all the nametags so they could sit together. Rosalee looked at Audra and just shook her head in amusement.

As soon as the clock struck six, Betty Hartford Hill stepped to the podium, pausing for everyone's attention. Millie had to admit, Betty looked chic. Her auburn hair was enhanced by the teal green dress she wore.

That must have set the mayor back a grand or two, she thought.

"Welcome, fellow classmates!" Betty called, clapping her hands. "It is so good to see all of you. I am Betty Hartford, now married to Wallace Hill, our town mayor. We love living here in our dear hometown, working constantly to make it a pleasant, safe place to live and raise children. We have two sons: Marcus, who is a banker; and Murphy, who is a lawyer."

She paused a moment to let the full effect of her sons' success filter through to everyone. "They and their beautiful wives have given us four adorable grandchildren."

Dan leaned over and whispered in Millie's ear, "Everybody knows she can't stand her daughters-in-law."

"Shush!" Millie elbowed him and gave him her most severe wifely look.

"I hope everyone will enjoy themselves tonight. This has been a dream of mine for quite some time, and with a *little* help from my friend Cora, and my husband the mayor, I have tried to make everything just perfect so that you will always remember it."

Betty continued, "Now, our classmate Norman Bellamy is our first speaker. He is going to share the list of our deceased former classmates. Then he will tell us about himself. After that, I will pull a name from the blue box, and that person will come tell us about him- or herself. As soon as that is all finished, our meal will be served, then we can mingle and dance... those who are still able."

After some obligatory laughter, Norman stepped to the podium in a bright blue suit, yellow shirt, and pink bow tie.

"My next Easter suit," Dan whispered to Millie, who gave him a glaring, yet amused, look.

"Good evening, fellow classmates. It is good to see everyone again. Unfortunately, after fifty years, several classmates are no longer with us. Among those is Shelby Hanes, who was killed in an automobile accident just six months after graduation. She had planned to be married in January, but died a month before her wedding. I remember Shelby with fondness. Next is Freddie Hearle, who was killed in Vietnam in nineteen sixty-seven. Freddie went straight from graduation to the Army. He was not married."

As he read each name, Norman lit a candle.

He continued, "Bobby Ganer, who died of colon cancer just four months ago, had a wife, four children, and eleven grandchildren. Bobby was a high school math teacher in Connecticut. I remember Bobby's sense of humor and his quick wit. Wanda Sallings was killed in a boating accident back in nineteen seventy-eight, leaving a husband and two children. Wanda worked in a finance office in Tennessee. Shirley Harwell died of ovarian cancer ten years ago. Shirley had a degree in engineering, and worked for a large corporation in St. Louis. She was married to an engineer, and they had no children. Carl Isleway, who was killed in a mining accident in nineteen sixty-eight, left a wife and one child behind. Jimmy Waynesly was killed in Vietnam, in nineteen sixty-nine. I have no other information on Jimmy. We are so thankful for our veterans, many of whom gave their lives for our freedom. Some of you here tonight may also be veterans; we thank you. Barry Hepling was another cancer victim, as was Brenda Mosley. There is no more information on either of them, except that Barry lived in Tennessee, and Brenda lived in Florida. Jackie Easton died from a heart attack in nineteen ninety-seven. He was a mechanic, with a wife, two children, and five grandchildren. They lived in Raleigh, North Carolina. Last is Charlotte Anderson, a wife and mother who died of congestive heart failure. May these dear classmates rest in peace; they will forever be in our hearts. At this time, I would like to ask Dan Cunningham to lead a prayer for our deceased."

After Dan delivered the prayer, Norman spoke again.

"It is good to be here with all of you tonight. Most of you remember me as Nerdy Norm, your high school class nerd. I guess the nerdiness has paid off, though. I am now *Doctor* Norman Bellamy; I am a doctor of microbiology at a well-known research center in Denver, Colorado. My wife and I have traveled a long distance for this reunion. Stella, my wife, is also a doctor of microbiology. Would you please stand, Stella?"

All eyes turned to see a tall, thin lady with white hair and dark-rimmed glasses, a perfect match for Nerdy Norm.

He continued. "We have no children, as our jobs are our life. I remember my high school days with fondness, and you as well. Thank you."

With straight shoulders and head held high, he walked back to his table and took his seat.

No children, thought Millie with a sigh. *How sad.*

Betty stepped back to the podium. "I wanted you to know that we sent a card of regret to a family member of each of our deceased classmates."

She drew out the next name. "Martha Jolings Pritchard."

A woman with blonde hair highlighted with purple streaks, wearing an abundance of makeup and four-inch spike heels, made her way precariously to the microphone.

"Good evening, my fellow classmates. It is hard to believe it's been fifty years since we walked across that little stage to receive our diplomas. I've only been back to Masonville twice since that day: once for my mother's funeral, and again for my father's funeral. Life just gets busy, doesn't it? My husband Dennis and I live in San Antonio, Texas, where we own a chain of warehouses that afford us a good living. Everyone, it seems, needs a warehouse these days."

She gave a little laugh, then continued, "We have no children together, but Dennis has two sons and a daughter by his first two marriages, and they have given him nine grandchildren. I keep busy with my bridge club and society groups. It is good to see all of you, and I hope to chat with everyone later."

Her classmates applauded courteously as she returned to her seat next to a balding, pot-bellied man.

His third wife? Millie silently pondered the matter. *Someone for everyone, I guess.*

Betty reached into the box and retrieved another name.

"Bunn Morris," she called.

This time everyone applauded loudly. They didn't know which one was Bunn, but they remembered their athletic star vividly.

Bunn arose and walked to the microphone, thankful for Marsha and her forceful weight loss regimen. He was also proud of his white swanee shirt, the one with the aqua palm trees.

"Goooood evening, fellow classmates!" he called out, to which everyone replied, "Goooood evening!"

The audience got quiet, waiting to see what their star football player had to say.

"I'm sure most of you remember the words of that old Statler Brothers song: 'Things get complicated when you get past eighteen.' Truer words were never spoken."

He paused and everyone waited in silence.

"I'm going to be quite honest with you," said Bunn, a calm, serious look on his face. "When I received the invitation to this reunion, I said, 'No way!'"

There was a moment of fidgeting, and if each face could have been seen, there would have been a blush of guilt on many of them. He'd just admitted what they had felt.

"Things got complicated, all right, and life did not turn out the way I'd planned it," continued Bunn. "I did not become a pro football player. I didn't become much of anything, and the blame is all mine. For a while, I was even homeless."

Audible gasps could be heard. Somewhere toward the back of the room, Willie Baker sat up a little straighter. Bunn was sharing some tough truths with his classmates.

He's a braver man than I am, Willie thought.

"I left here angry at some things in my home life, and real high on my own abilities. That's not the best medicine for success, as I soon found out. Pride always leads to a fall. I flunked out of college and lost my scholarship. I thought they would never fail a football star, but the joke was on me. I was rescued by a man by the name of Pastor Bob. He took me in when I was starving, fed me, clothed me, gave me a job, and taught me about the love of Jesus Christ. He made me feel worthwhile again. I entered into a marriage that barely lasted until the ink on the license dried, and I have a daughter I have never seen."

Willie Baker sat up even straighter. *What guts that guy has!*

By this time everyone was listening intently. Was this their football star talking, the hunk of the class of '65?

"After the marriage failure, I moved to Chicago, where I met a man who owned a bar and grill. He took me under his wing, and just before he died, sold me the bar and grill for a pittance. I still own it, and it does quite well. I have folks working for me who could easily run the place by themselves. They are my family, the only family I have, and they are the reason I finally accepted the invitation to this reunion. They believed in me when I didn't believe in myself. I must also confess to you that, a few months ago, I weighed three hundred and twenty-seven pounds."

Another audible gasp filled the room. Willie listened in astonishment as Bunn revealed these things to the entire audience, but mingled with the astonishment, Willie felt pride in his old classmate and a new strength in himself.

"You see, fellow classmates, life does not always turn out the way we plan, but it is usually what we make it. We have to decide what is important in life. I know most of you have been wiser than I have been, but the thing I hope most is that you are happy. We can have millions and be unhappy, and we can have little and be filled with joy and happiness. I just wanted to be honest with you tonight, in case any of you are struggling with what is important in life. It is wonderful to see all of you again and to return to Masonville, our little hometown. Returning was a good decision."

As he left the podium, everyone in the audience stood and applauded loudly. A few wiped their eyes. Several shook Bunn's hand as he made his way back to his table. They had heard honesty, and they admired Bunn for that even more than they had admired his athletic ability.

Willie Baker puffed his cheeks and blew out air in relief.

Once again there was quiet, as they waited for Betty to draw the next name. For a moment, she sat as if in a trance; then she arose slowly and walked to the box. Pulling out a name, she announced in a quivering voice, "Mabel Perkins Beck."

All eyes turned to see just what Mabel Perkins looked like. Then eyes widened.

Making her way between tables and up to the podium was a round little lady with dark red hair, purple dress, red hat, huge red and purple earrings, and a shoe of each color.

"Hello! Hello! Hello! My name is Mabel Perkins Beck, and if you haven't figured it out already, I'm a member of the Red Hat Society! We are just a bunch of ladies who love life and know how to enjoy it. Life is short, so we make the most of it in our good clean way. If you are a stuffed shirt, get over it! Have some fun!

"As you may remember, in our senior year I was voted Wittiest Girl. I just about dropped my drawers when I was chosen, 'cause I always considered myself of a serious nature."

At this, several laughed.

"Now, Bucky Edwards truly deserved Wittiest Boy. Why, he even looked witty! I think he was born that way. His mother said the first time she laid eyes on him, she knew the Lord had played a joke on her."

More laughter filled the room.

"I'm here tonight with my husband Arnold. Hi, Arnie!" She gave him a little wave.

"Actually, he's my third husband. My first husband couldn't leave the women alone, and the second one couldn't leave the booze alone. I always say I was married to a drinker and a stinker."

The crowd broke into peals of laughter. Mabel continued without taking a breath. Some noticed that Betty Hartford sat over to the left, hand over her heart, with a combined look of amusement and astonishment.

"Now, Arnold isn't a thing like that. He gets a little contrary sometimes, and then I call him Ornery Arnold. He said the other day, 'Mabel, darling...'—I like it when he calls me that—he said 'Mabel, darling, why don't you join a book club or the historical society instead of those Red Hat Ladies?' Can you see me in a stuffy ole historical society? I'd die from frowning, and I don't like frown lines. Now, if they ever start a *hysterical* society, I might consider it."

By this point, her classmates were rolling with laughter.

"You all look a lot better when you laugh. Of course, from what I've seen so far tonight, there was nowhere for you to go but up!"

Handkerchiefs were out now, wiping tears of laughter. Betty Hartford Hill had her handkerchief out too, but she was using it to fan her flushed face.

"I saw Martin Henry earlier. Where are you, Martin?"

She shaded her eyes with her hand.

"You know he was named Most Intellectual. I thought he deserved it...'til one day he was filling out some papers, and asked me how to spell *intellectual*. I spelled it wrong, just to be messin' with him. At least he was able to find his way here tonight. I didn't much like him in school because he always knew the answers, but we had a little talk and he promised not to be a know-it-all tonight.

"I do have some atoning to do. First, I have to atone for putting a frog in Harpo Hunter's locker. None of us knew Harpo had such a set of lungs. Miss Mueller didn't have a sense of humor, I guess. She grabbed him by the ear and took him to the office. I hear he got a week of in-school suspension for raising such a ruckus. Thank goodness nobody thought to ask how the frog got there. I talked to Harpo earlier and asked his forgiveness. 'Mabel,' he said, 'if we end up in the same place after the rapture, I'll forgive you.'

To which I replied, 'Harpo, I'm a good southern Baptist, and I've got eternal security. If you don't have it, you better be gettin' it.'"

The handkerchiefs were still wiping.

"Of course, I can't atone to Mr. Crawford. They tell me he has already crossed the river. I hope I had nothing to do with that. Remember when I put that jar of ladybugs in his desk drawer? I thought, being a science teacher, he'd be able to take care of the little critters. But while he was teaching, he opened his drawer to get a pen, and them little critters decided to set themselves free. I forgot to put a lid on the jar, and there's nothing like thirty emancipated ladybugs. While he was explaining the fauna of the area, one little ladybug decided to light on his ear. He didn't seem to feel it, so no one said anything. Then as he was naming some of the fauna, two of the little darlings lit on his tie. Some of you began to twitter. I thought it was kinda cute. Then, as he switched to talking about the flora of the area, two more lit in his hair. That's when he began to notice...and when he looked down in the desk drawer. It was about that time, too, when his face took on that bright red color. Thank God the bell rang! We all hurried out of there without looking back. Well, I glanced real quick like. He was swatting ladybugs left and right, and his mouth was moving. I'm pretty good at reading lips, and the words I read weren't too pretty."

By this time there wasn't a dry eye in the entire audience.

"Oh, I forgot to mention what we do for a living. Arnold is the pastor of a large church, and I'm the choir director."

A stunned silence spread through the room.

"Naw! I'm just messin' with you! We own a little restaurant in Montville, Tennessee."

The laughter came again as people shook their heads.

"Well, I've talked long enough. Old Ornery Arnold is pointing to his watch. Y'all keep smilin', 'cause those frown wrinkles are downright ugly. By the way, let's have us a seventy-five-year reunion!"

As Mabel made her way back to Old Arnold, everyone stood and applauded. She had made their night just a little better.

Even Betty Hill was smiling as she walked to the box to draw another name.

"Audra James!"

With nervous hesitation, Audra walked slowly to the platform. Every eye was on her and as she passed by one table, she heard someone say "Wow! How young she looks!"

She stepped to the podium and took a deep breath.

"It is good to see all of you tonight. Most of you remember me as the preacher's daughter. I was not a social part of the class of sixty-five; in fact, I was downright mousey. The truth is, my father did not allow me to socialize. Being a preacher's daughter can be a difficult life when the preacher is as mean as my father was. But we won't dwell on my father. I left Masonville with relief and good riddance two days after graduation, and ended up in Michigan where I worked at various jobs. I met a woman who was on her way to a new job in New York City, and she invited me to come along. She volunteered to share her apartment until I could afford one of my own. I soon found a job in a real estate office as a file clerk. The job was my life, and I was always volunteering to work overtime. I guess the owners of the agency took this to be dedication, and I quickly moved up. For the last thirty years, I have been head secretary to the owner of the real estate agency. It is a wonderful job, but it's still my life; I've never married. I almost didn't come tonight. Masonville holds some bad memories for me, but I'm glad I came. It was good to see you all again, and to put certain things behind me. It was especially good to see one old friend again, and to meet some new ones. Thank you."

As she said the last words, she looked at Willie, then at Harm, Rosalee, and Bunn. Everyone applauded as she returned to their table.

Betty pulled out the next name. "Harmon Cline."

Harm walked to the podium.

"Good evening, everyone. As some others have confessed, I didn't plan to attend this reunion, but my wife Rosalee convinced me to come. I have some wonderful memories of this school...of the basketball court, the football field, and the baseball field. I loved sports. I even have good memories of some of my teachers. There were some bad memories, however, and I spent many years running from them, but some time in Vietnam can make anything look good. I have met some old friends in the past few days, and they have made my decision to return a good one. I live in Michigan with my wife Rosalee, where I own and operate a trucking firm. Someone asked me when I plan to retire, but when you love what you do, you just want to keep at it as long as you can. It is good to see all of you."

As Harm walked back to his seat, he was a little surprised at himself. He had come here planning to let them all know of his success and that he was worth millions. After coming back, though, it just didn't seem important anymore. He was happy. That was the important thing. He had Rosalee, and he had renewed some old friendships. You just couldn't buy that with money.

Betty read the next name. "Zeta Moss Ellings."

Everyone waited as a frail little lady with white hair carefully arose, reached for her walker, and slowly made her way to the stage. Betty handed the microphone down to her from the podium, and she turned to speak.

"I know, most of you were feeling sorry for me as I made my way up here. Let me set your mind at rest. I do have handicaps, and movement is not easy, but rest assured, I have had an amazing life, and I couldn't wait to see all of you. My husband Charles and I drove down yesterday from Kentucky. It was so good to drive through this town one more time, and to see my old school once again."

There was a slight quiver in Zeta's voice as she spoke.

"I was diagnosed eight years ago with Parkinson's Disease. It was not a pleasant diagnosis to hear. We all know the outcome. Then one day, I realized we all have that outcome, in one way or another. That's when I decided to make the most of the life I have remaining. I have been blessed with the best husband God had to offer. He is always there for me, never complaining, eager to help me in any way I need. We have four children: two sons and two daughters. They are also helpful and encouraging. Before the Parkinson's, I worked for a newspaper, and I loved my job. God has been good to me. It is good to be here with all of you, my dear classmates. By the way, Mabel, I remember those ladybugs, and I actually heard a few of the words Mr. Crawford said...God rest his soul."

Betty once more drew from the box. "Cora Mae Davis."

Cora Mae stepped to the podium, a shyness in her demeanor. Her hair was pulled tightly back from her face and fastened with a clip. She wore only the faintest hint of makeup.

Her figure is actually quite nice, thought Millie Cunningham as Cora took the microphone from Betty. *I wonder why she always seems to be afraid of everyone.*

"Good evening, my fellow classmates." Her voice was soft. "It is wonderful to see each of you, and to talk with you after so many years. I have thoroughly enjoyed preparing for this reunion with Betty. I am the librarian at the Masonville Public Library, a job I truly enjoy. In September, I will celebrate my forty-eighth year there. I have never married. Until two years ago, I took care of my ailing mother for several years. The people of our little town are my family, and I especially enjoy the children as they come into the library. I try to impart to them the joy and importance of reading. My life, I'm sure, would seem boring and empty to many, but it is the life I have chosen and the life I love, May God richly bless each of you."

As everyone clapped, Cora Mae walked meekly back to her seat. Only Betty saw the little smile she gave someone.

One by one, the classmates told their stories. It was interesting to hear just where life had taken each one. After each had spoken, the meal was served and then everyone mingled and talked. A few danced. Harm found a moment to speak privately to Willie.

"Willie, I need to talk with you. Could we do that later tonight when everyone turns in?"

"Sure, man," replied Willie, a perplexed look on his face.

They all lingered another hour, then left with plans to meet at a little coffee shop that kept late hours.

"Now, aren't you all glad you came?" asked Rosalee, as they sat around the café table.

"Yes, Rosalee. I'm extremely glad," answered Bunn. "I think we all faced our ghosts and got rid of some baggage tonight. I feel like I can look at life in a more positive manner. It was good to hear about everyone's life. We've all had our share of problems. Wasn't that Zeta Moss something? Talk about strength and a positive attitude..."

"Are you heading back to Chicago tomorrow?" asked Harm.

"No, I don't think so. Not for a few more days."

"You look like you have something in mind," said Willie.

"Well, I guess I do. I want to go back by to see my Aunt Jenny, and Ms. Sophie. I promised them I would. Then I'm going to try to find my daughter. I owe her an apology. She most likely won't want anything to do with me, but I need to tell her how sorry I am. I'm not even sure I can find her, but I have to try. It's shameful that I don't even know her name. I've made so many mistakes in my life, and it's time I atone for some of them."

Rosalee reached over and put her hand on his. "I think that's a wonderful plan, Bunn."

"You know, we all need to get together from time to time," said Harm. "Friends are important, as I have found out in the past few days. What do you say?"

"I say *yes*," answered Bunn, smiling.

Willie and Audra remained quiet.

"What do you think, Willie?" asked Bunn, noticing his silence.

Willie's face held sadness. "Bunn, I think it's a great idea. I just don't know if I can afford to travel until I get a better job, but if I can, I most definitely would like to get together with everyone."

"What about you, Audra?" asked Bunn.

Audra smiled. "Yes. I would like to get together. I just want Willie to be with us, too."

They talked on awhile and then everyone decided to call it a night. Only Harm and Willie remained. Both were tired, so Harm got right to the point.

"Willie, you know I used to take a lot of ribbing because I didn't have a father, or at least, didn't know who he was."

"Yeah, Harm. That was pretty bad, but then I had a father and wished many times I didn't."

Harm sat quietly for a moment, thinking. Willie knew something was seriously bothering him, but he waited for Harm to speak again.

"It was always important to me to know who my father was, but my mother would never tell me. He had married and had a family, and she didn't want to interfere in any way. But I was young and headstrong; one night when she was working late, I went through some things in her room. I found some letters that told me who my father was. I never told anyone about it, not even

137

my mom. These are the letters."

"Do you want me to read your mother's letters?" questioned Willie, as Harm pushed the letters over to him. Harm simply nodded, so Willie began to read.

After the third letter, Willie looked up, studying Harm's face. Then he continued to read. Each letter was signed by a first name only. The name was *Ferrell*.

"Do these say what I think they say?"

"Yes, Willie. I believe your father was also my father. I believe we are brothers."

"But he never signs his last name."

"No, but once he adds his last initial, B. See, on this one. It's signed *Ferrell B.* How many Ferrell B's were there in Masonville?"

"Man!" That was all Willie could get out.

"What do you think about the whole thing?" asked Harm.

"I don't know. There's no one I would rather have as a brother, but look at you and look at me. You are at least six feet five or more, and I'm a shrimp. Can it be?"

"From all the pictures I've seen, I take after my mother's side," said Harm. "They were all pretty tall. My mom was five-ten. Your dad was barely that. We can do a DNA test, but I don't have any doubts."

"The letters pretty much make it official," said Willie, shaking his head. "Do you think that's why my father was always so mean to me? Do you think he resented me because he didn't have the life he wanted? That would sure explain a lot of things. I just can't quite take it in."

"I don't think he ever knew about me," said Harm. "The letters give no indication of that. Of course, there could have been other letters, but my gut tells me he never knew."

Willie sat in silence, waiting for Harm to continue.

"Willie, I own a large trucking firm, as I have mentioned. What I didn't say is that it is worth millions. I want you to come help me run it."

"What?"

"Notice, I didn't say 'come work for me.' I said I want you to come help me run it. I need to put in less hours and with a good partner, I could cut back. Oh, it would take a while for you to learn the ropes, but I don't think it would take all that long. Why don't you go back and work off your parole, and then move to Michigan? I'll find you a nice apartment, or even a house; it could be ready and waiting for you."

"I can't grasp all of this, Harm," said Willie, his voice almost a whisper. "Why would you want to do this for me? You don't owe me anything just because of what you discovered in the letters."

"Willie, that's what a brother is for. Truth is, I need a family. I never had anyone but my mother. Something was always missing. What do you say? We may still have many good years left in us, and we've got a great deal in common besides being brothers."

"Let me mull this over tonight; I'll give you an answer before we leave tomorrow. I just need a little time to let this all sink in. But Harm, I don't want any handouts. I want only what I earn."

"Understood," agreed Harm.

The two men embraced. "We'll talk more tomorrow," said Harm, his voice cracking.

The next morning, they all met for coffee and bagels one last time. Bunn was going to visit Ms. Sophie and his Aunt Jenny, then set out on the search for his daughter.

"Call me when you get us another get-together planned," he told them.

Harm gave him a firm handshake. "You'll hear from us much sooner than that, my friend."

Rosalee looked at Harm, who gave her a slight nod, and she turned to Audra. "Audra, let's you and me take a little walk and let the guys talk, OK?"

Audra looked at her, then Willie, a question in her eyes. "Sounds good."

After they left, Harm turned to Willie. "Well, my brother?"

"I've decided to take you up on your offer. I don't see how I can turn down a chance to make something out of my life, plus have a brother, too. I will have to finish my parole first, but I can come pretty soon. I don't even own enough to pack. I can hitch a ride and be there in a day, probably."

"No way!" said Harm. "I'm getting you a plane ticket. I have this for you, too."

He handed Willie a cellphone.

"What's this for?"

"This is so we can keep in touch and make our plans."

Willie took the phone.

"There's one more thing I have to do, Harm. I have to tell Audra about all this. I'm hoping she might come to Michigan with me. There was no way before that I could ask her to share my life, but now I can. She may turn me down, but I've got to try."

"From what I've seen in that woman's eyes, she won't turn you down," said Harm. "I like Audra, Willie, and I want to see you happy."

A few minutes later Rosalee and Audra returned from their walk, and Harm and Rosalee said their good-byes.

"I'll see you in a few months, brother," he said to Willie. "I'll have everything ready."

Audra looked at them with confusion as they said their good-byes.

Then it was just the two of them. "What did Harm mean, Willie?"

Willie told her the story of the letters, and that he and Harm were half-brothers. She quietly listened in amazement. "It seems we are half-brothers, although I still can't grasp the whole thing. Harm has no doubt, though."

"It sounds like a fairy tale, Willie."

"There's more, though, Audra. That's what I wanted to talk to you about. Harm wants me to finish my parole time and then move to Michigan. He wants to take me in as a partner, to help run his business. It's not just a small firm, Audra. It's worth millions. I could finally make something of myself."

Tears fell from Audra's eyes. "That is absolutely wonderful, Willie. I'm so very happy for you."

"It doesn't have to be just for me, Audra."

"What do you mean?"

"Audra, I have loved you since ninth grade, and seeing you again has confirmed for me that I still do. Do you think you could ever be happy with me? I know I'm not much to look at, and my life hasn't been pretty. Then there are the nightmares I may always have, but we could have a good life; I promise I would love you forever."

Audra sat quietly for several moments. Willie's hope began to fade. *She's going to say no...*

"Willie, I love you, too. I just have so much fear when it comes to relationships, and I'm afraid I couldn't make you happy. I'm damaged from my past."

"No one could make me happier than you, Audra. We are both damaged from the past. Let's help each other to heal. What do you say?"

"I say, OK!"

"OK? Does that mean you will marry me?"

"That's exactly what it means. Let's do this, Willie: You go back and finish your parole and move on out to Michigan. I'll go back to my job. If, after you begin work with Harm, you still want me, I will come without delay. How's that?"

"Oh, I'll still want you. You have no reason for doubt. Finally, Audra, we can have a good life. This is the first time in my life I have felt there is real hope. Pastor Ben always said we have to wait on God's timing. You know, this was one great class reunion!"

They decided to drive around town one more time before they headed their separate ways. As they passed the old school, they held hands. As they passed the little soda shop, they were still holding hands, and as they crossed the railroad track, their hands were still together and in each heart was a joy and peace they had never known before.

We Came!
We Saw!
We Conquered!!!

The reunion wasn't just a one-night event. For many, it was a turning point. Some faced their ghosts, some found renewal, some strutted their stuff, and some realized what is important in life.

Betty Hartford Hill felt important that night. For one night, she was a star. The reunion had been perfect; everyone had thanked her and told her what a fantastic job she had done. She accepted the praise with false modesty. Betty's life changed drastically two weeks later, when Wallace and Cora Mae ran off together. He called her from Reno to tell her he was getting a divorce and would not return to Masonville. She heard the words Poor Betty once again, but this time it was in *support* of her instead of the ridicule that had once accompanied the name. The only complaints were from her daughters-in-law, who bewailed the humiliation they had to endure.

Murphy's wife called her on the phone a few days after Wallace and Cora Mae took flight. Her voice had that whininess Betty hated.

"Mother Hill, how are we ever going to be able to hold our heads up in this town? How could Father Hill do this to us?"

Betty summoned all the dislike she had felt for her daughter-in-law over the years and said simply, "Elaina, can it!" It felt so good to say that!

Actually, Betty came out pretty well. Masonville had no mayor. Guess who the town appointed as the new mayor? You guessed it! Betty now runs the town *officially*.

Each night before going to bed, she takes a sip of wine and silently thanks Cora Mae for her new life.

You can see Millie Davis Cunningham and Dan out walking early every morning. Not jogging, just walking. Millie decided she liked exercise after all...well, some of it. Sometimes they even hold hands. I hear there's a *For Sale* sign in Dan Cunningham's hardware store, and two people have already made offers. Rumor has it that Dan is ready to retire, and a little trip to Hawaii is on the agenda. No, they haven't bought a beach house yet, but the girls are still working on them.

Bunn Wilson went to see Aunt Jenny and Ms. Sophie before leaving Masonville, as promised. He took Ms. Sophie a beautiful potted geranium, sipped lemonade with her on the porch, and told her all about the reunion. She loved the story about the ladybugs.

"How can critters so lovely be so pesky?" she asked laughing.

Aunt Jenny was glad to see him once more, and loved the fresh red roses he gave her. She was thrilled that Bunn had renewed acquaintance with some of his high school friends, and that they were going to keep in touch. The change in her nephew was obvious. Aunt Jenny was also glad he was going to search for his daughter.

"Maybe I'll live to hear that you have found her. Wouldn't that be just hunky dory?"

Bunn laughed. "You'll be the first to hear the news, Aunt Jenny. That's a promise."

He left with another promise: to call Aunt Jenny once a week.

Bunn didn't find his daughter...at least not yet. He hasn't given up, though. His ex-wife had moved from the place where she had lived when their daughter was born, and Bunn had no way of knowing what her married name was. He's still following clues, searching records and making use of the internet. He did find out his daughter's first name is Marianne; can't be more than fifty thousand Mariannes in the world. In the meantime, he's taking a little more time off and letting Marsha, Ray, and Gid run things. He has learned to text, so he hears from the guys at least once a week. (There's a lot to be said for these new-fangled gadgets.) He was surprised to hear about Harm and Willie being brothers, but he was happy for them. They're all going to get together soon for some new announcement. Bunn has an idea what that's all about. There's still hope in this ole world.

Willie Baker finished his parole; even got a nice write-up from his parole officer. He enjoyed handing in his two-weeks notice at the warehouse. He's already in Michigan and living in a nice new apartment that has no mice or rats—and he eats *good* food, no moldy bread. Working with Harm is a joy. It isn't easy work, but it allows a man to go home feeling good at night. He goes bowling with Harm and Rosalee every Friday night, and to church with them on Sundays and Wednesday nights. He also keeps in touch with Pastor Ben and Bear. They have even promised to come up for the wedding. Guess who is performing the ceremony?!

Audra James will soon be joining Willie. She just has some business matters to attend to first. Though no one would guess it, she is actually well-off financially. When you work thirty-odd years at a good job and seldom spend anything, it adds up; Audra feels good that she has something to offer to the marriage. She also has an idea running around in her head, created by what she remembers Bunn and Willie talking about: being homeless, and being helped by some people who cared. It's just an idea, but maybe she could build a place like that. Maybe Willie's friend Pastor Ben could offer some ideas. First though, she has to get moved. Then there's a wedding to plan. It will be small, no white dress and veil, but it will be in Harm and Rosalee's church, and she's hoping Bunn can come for it.

Never thought I'd be planning a wedding, mused Audra, smiling in satisfaction. *Never thought I'd find happiness. I may even get on speaking terms with Jesus. Willie seems to like him pretty well.*

Nobody has heard any more from Mabel Perkins Beck, but wherever she is, she's definitely wearing her red hat. Maybe she's even writing a book about her shenanigans at Masonville High. Hope Old Ornery Arnold is surviving.

Sadly, Sybil Perkins Beck passed away just eight months after the reunion. Arthur said one minute she was laughing, and the next she was grabbing her chest. He said she died happy, though. Something had changed in both of them the week of the reunion. After her death, Arthur sold everything and moved back to Evanston, as they had planned, to be near Charlie. Rumor has it he bought out Mrs. Marshall's part in Happy Hearts Village, as she wanted to retire, and he and Charlie are seen often at McDonalds eating Big Macs and telling knock-knock-jokes. I hear also that Arthur is teaching Charlie to play golf...when Charlie has time away from his flowers, that is. They have to be hummed to, you know.

The Class of '65 had quite a reunion. There's one thing I've learned folks: God has a plan and He has His own timing...and it ain't over 'til it's over. *Go to that next reunion!*

Life gets complicated when we get past eighteen...

But don't ever give up your dreams.

We're gonna fight, fight, fight, For dear old Masonville! We're gonna win this game; You're doggone right we will! For the great old school we love so well, We're gonna win, win, yell, yell...Masonville!

Sometimes it's good
to stop and look back
After crossing that
old railroad track.
There are more rails
behind us than ahead;
We're getting old,
but we're not dead.
There's life to live
and life to share;
Chances to take
if we only dare.
Now we're looking ahead,
not looking back,
Chugging down a
brand new railroad track.

Honaker High School Class of '65:
I hope you remember the railroad track!

Questions for the Reader

1. When you think back to your elementary school days, what is the first thing that comes to your mind?
2. When you think back to your high school days, what is the first thing that comes to your mind?
3. Who was your most memorable elementary teacher? Why?
4. What were you most afraid of in elementary school?
5. Did you ever get a "spanking"? Did you deserve it?
6. Who was your most memorable high school teacher? Why?
7. What dream did you have in high school that you are glad did not come true?
8. Without too much thought, name five special classmates.
9. We all have some regrets. Do you have one regret that stands out about your high school days?
10. If you could go back to your high school days, what is one thing you would change about yourself?

About the Author

 Brenda Crissman Musick considers herself a true product of the Appalachians, a place that holds her heart. It is where she belongs. She loves sitting on her front porch, watching the cows and their young across the road, listening to the bluebirds, cardinals, mockingbirds, and robins serenade her. She even enjoys the raucous calls of the crows and blue jays as she sits and reads or works crossword puzzles, waving at neighbors as they pass. She loves the people, the friendliness, and the natural beauty of the area.

Her childhood was a time of lightheartedness, of learning, and of growing. At the same time, it was a slower-paced life and a life of hard work. She hoed corn and tobacco, pulled weeds out of those darn onions, and helped can in the summer and fall. She was taught to appreciate the area and to respect it. It was a time of imagination; a time of true socialization when you really saw the people and the surroundings.

School was an important time of her life, as she loved learning, especially writing and literature. Honaker High School holds precious memories for her. She graduated in 1965 and later received a Bachelor of Science in Education from UVA-Wise. Teaching elementary and middle school was a highlight of her life, arousing students' enthusiasm for novels, writing, poetry, and even mythology.

Today, Brenda and her husband of fifty-four years, enjoy the quiet life on their little farm in the Big A Mountain section of Honaker. They also enjoy the not so quiet life when all their children and grandchildren come to visit. They enjoy their church and church family. Life is good. God is good.

Other Books by Brenda Crissman Musick

A Trilogy: The Trials of an Appalachian Family

Young girls of the Appalachian Mountains had their dreams...simple dreams of marrying a good man, moving across the hill and raising a family. Carrie Ranes had those dreams, and for a while it seemed her dreams had come true. She had a husband, a home, and children...but Tom had a restlessness in him and a roving eye...

Tom's children have suffered greatly for his sins, but after eight years Luke is returning home, searching for a place to belong. Jessie is searching for happiness, but can he trust himself to ever be a husband? What if he's like his father? Alice has lost so much in her life. Is she going to lose even more?

The years have passed and it seems the Swank family has finally put the pain and shame behind them. But it's not yet the season for peace. In fact, an entire town suffers because of One-Eyed Tom's sins. But Carrie and her children have something Tom never had; they have their love and their faith to see them through the seasons of life.

A collection of stories and poems about growing up in the country, many from the author's own life. Some stories will make the reader laugh; others will bring tears, but each one will take you to the country.

www.ingramcontent.com/pod-product-compliance
Lightning Source LLC
Chambersburg PA
CBHW030128260626
47156CB00008B/2849